DC™ SUPER-PETS!

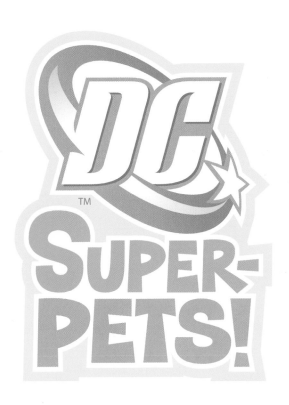

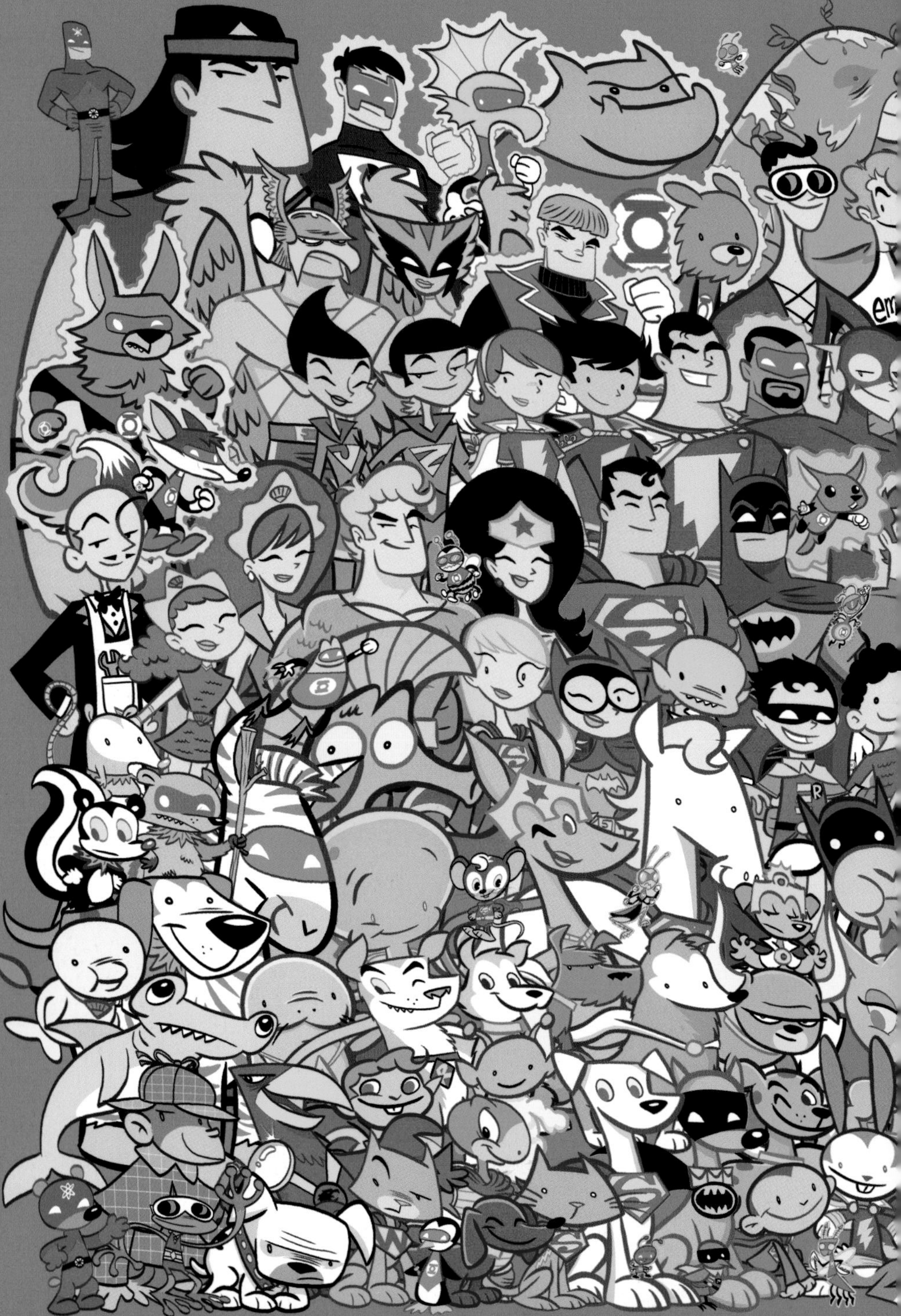

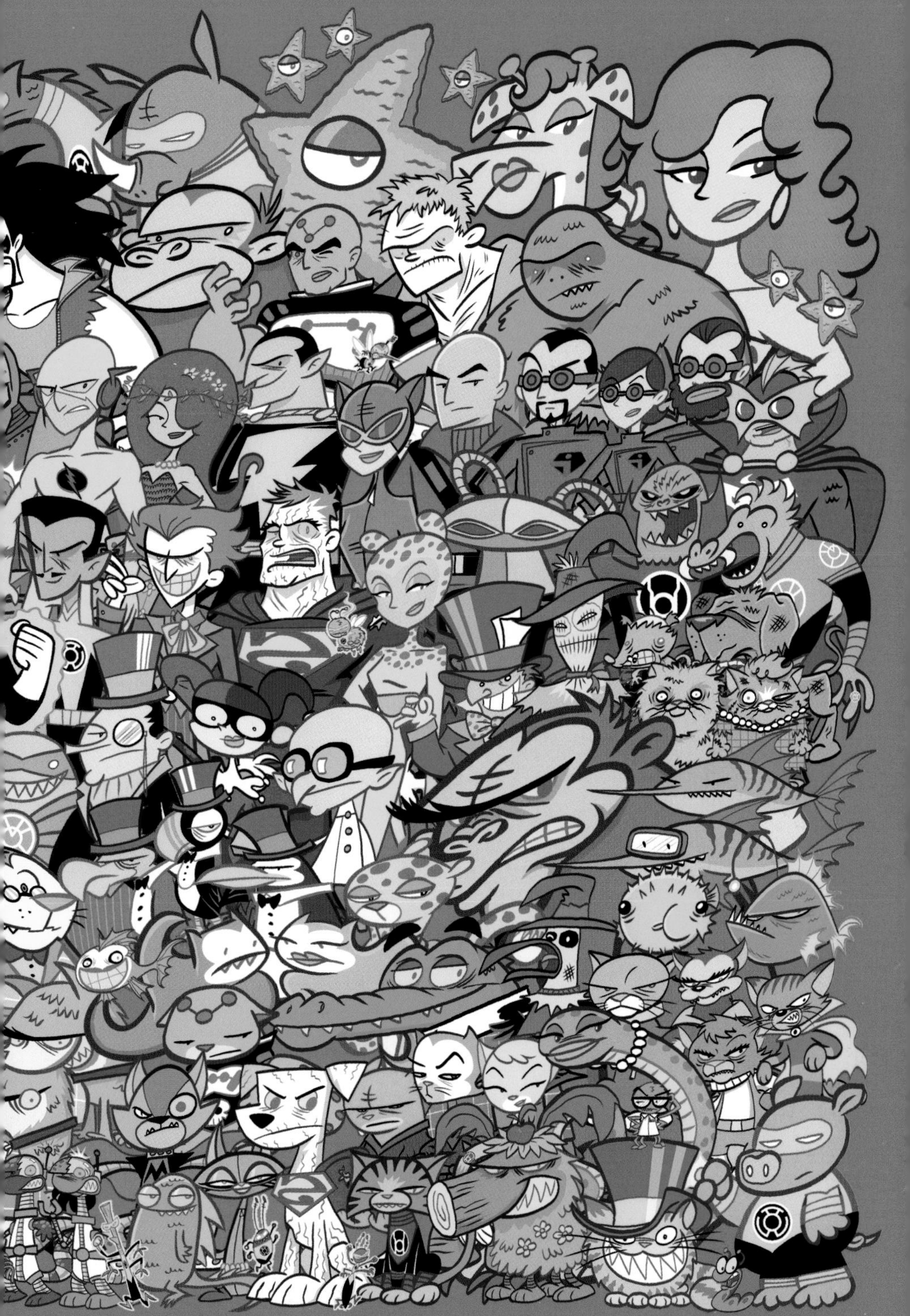

DC™

SUPER-PETS!

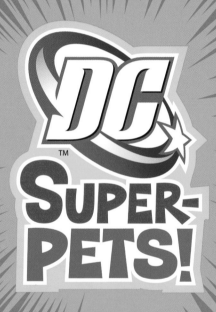

by Michael Dahl

THE FANTASTIC
FLEXY FROG!

illustrated by
Art Baltazar

Plastic Man created by Jack Cole

Picture Window Books
a capstone imprint

Starring...

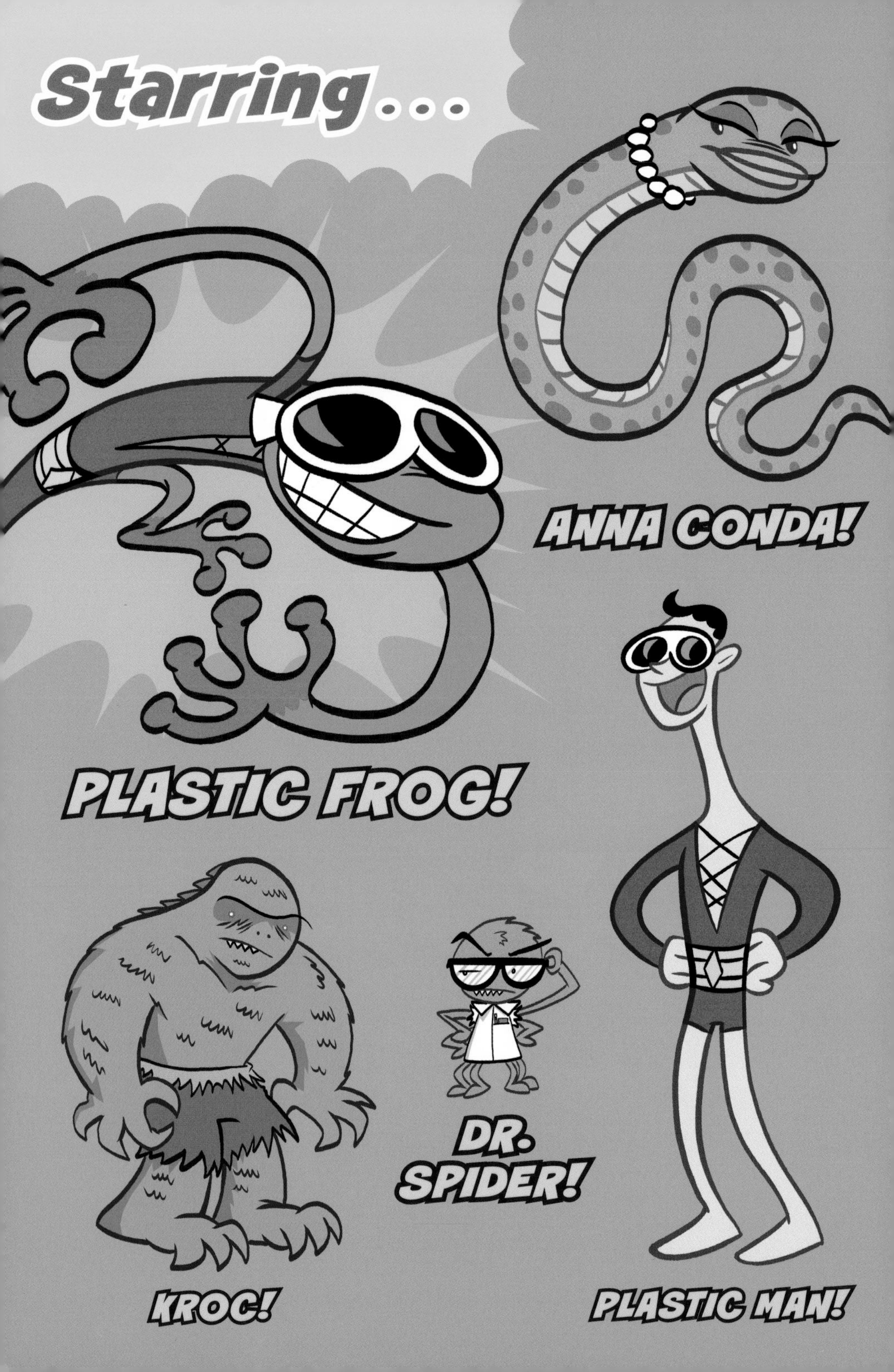
ANNA CONDA!
PLASTIC FROG!
DR. SPIDER!
KROC!
PLASTIC MAN!

TABLE OF CONTENTS!

Plastic Man COMPUTER

SUPER-PET HERO FILE 021:
PLASTIC FROG

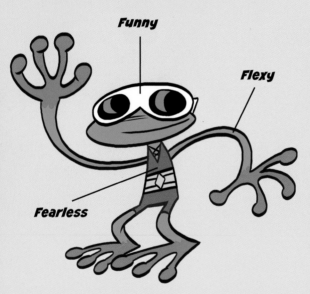

Funny

Flexy

Fearless

Super Hero Owner:
PLASTIC MAN

Species: Flexy Frog

Place of Birth: Costa Tico

Age: Unknown

Favorite Food: Fruit Flies

Bio: This fearless amphibian goes to great lengths in fighting crime, always bouncing back for more!

4

Super-Pet Enemy File 021:
DR. SPIDER

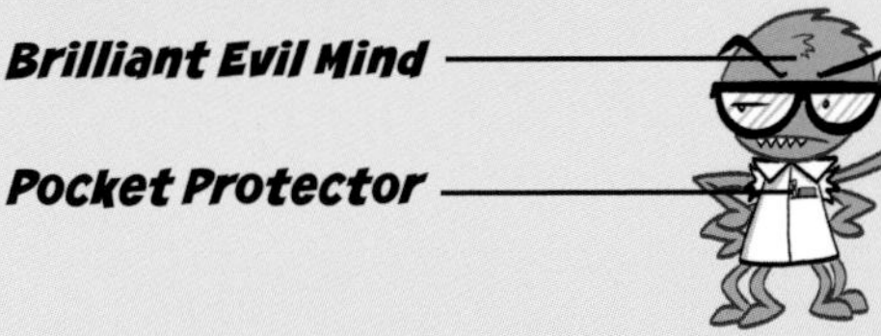
Brilliant Evil Mind
Pocket Protector

Super-Pet Enemy File 021B:
ANNA CONDA

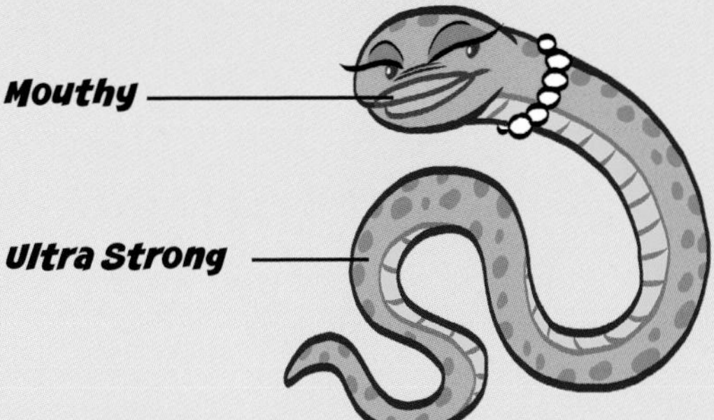
Mouthy
Ultra Strong

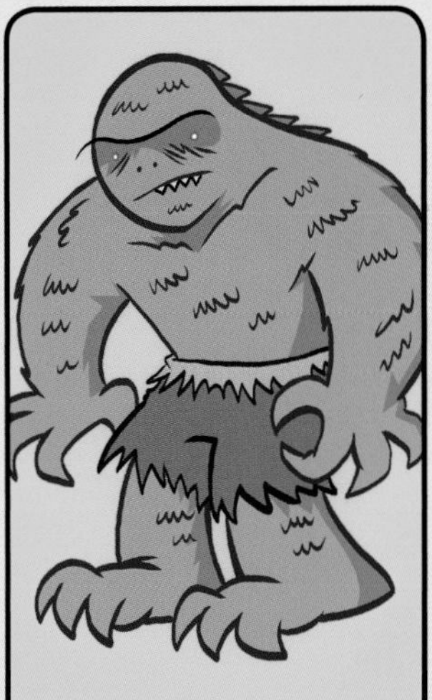

Super-villain Owner:
KROC

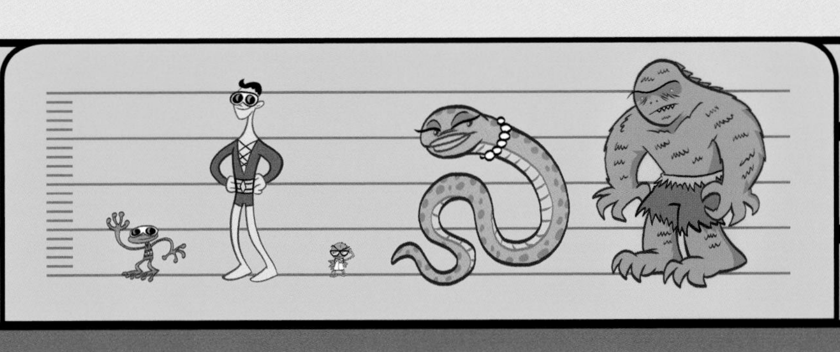

Chapter 1

GONE-AWAY LAGOON

The sun was shining brightly above the beaches of Costa Tico. The sky was blue, and the sand was gold. And **Plastic Man** was turning bright red. His face and hands and legs were starting to match his super hero uniform. But he didn't care.

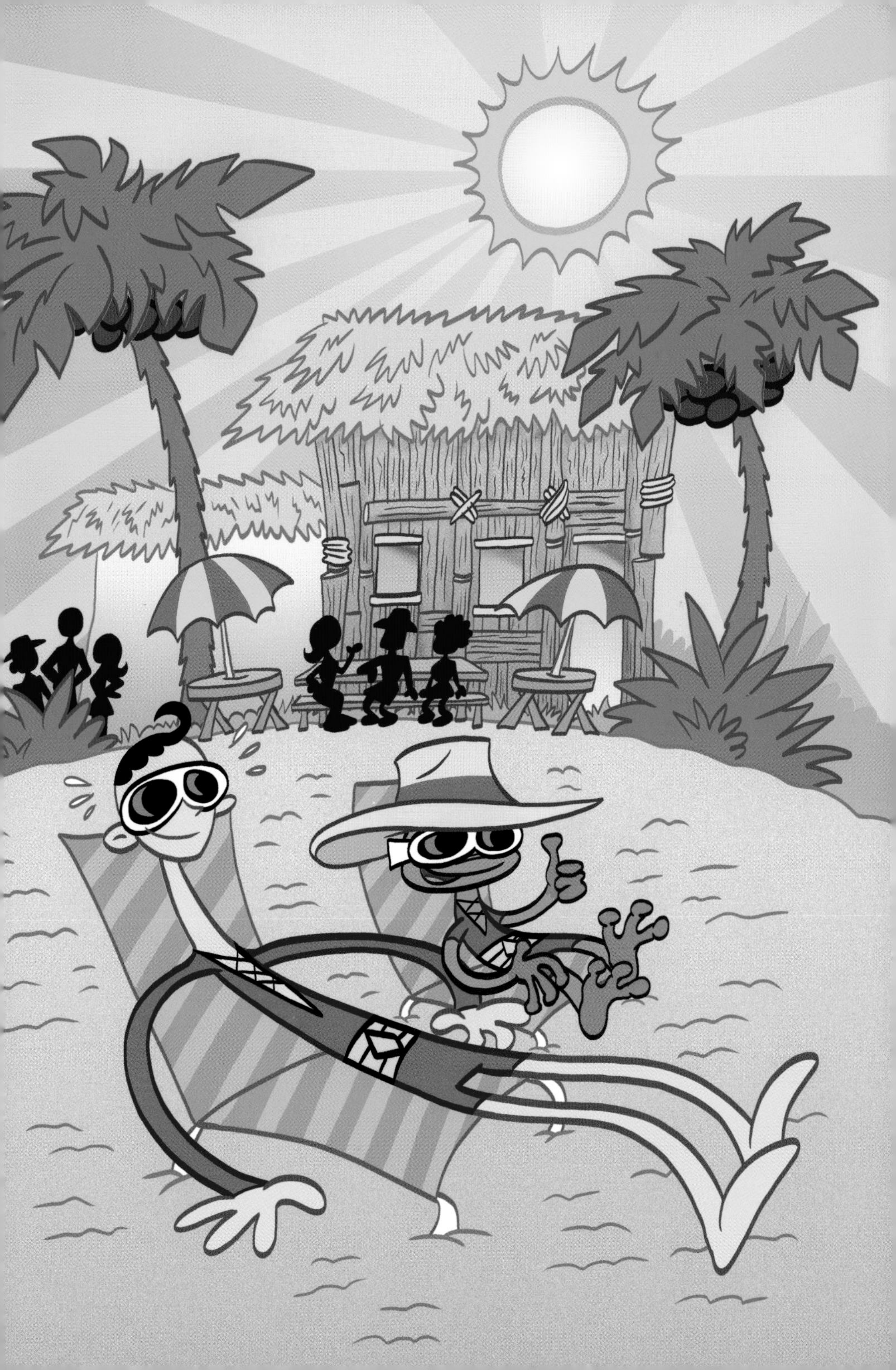

“What a perfect day!” said Plastic Man. “And a perfect vacation spot.”

“And a perfect sunburn,” added Plastic Frog. ZING! His fingers stretched around their chairs and pointed at his friend’s face.

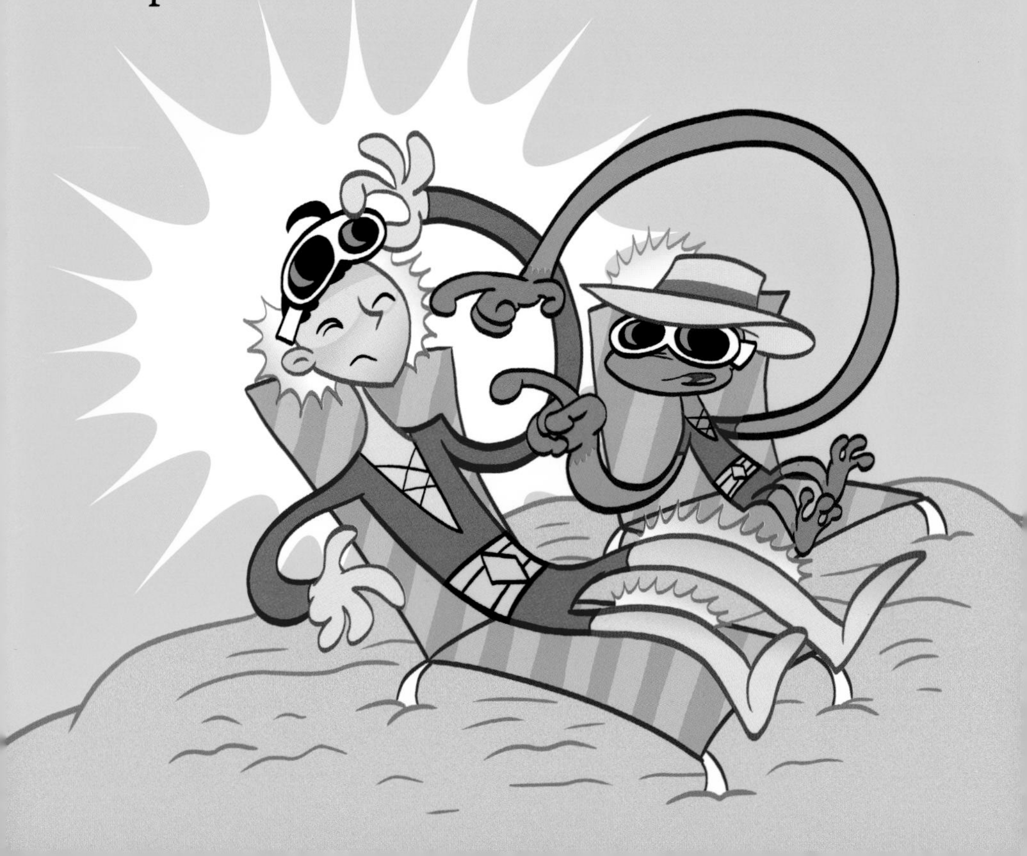

The little flexy frog and Plastic Man both had the same powers. They could flex their bodies into amazing shapes.

"No problemo," said Plastic Man. "I'll just reach into my hotel room for more suntan lotion and — **Ouch!"**

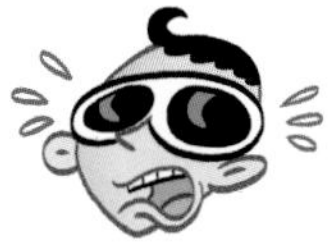

Plastic Man stretched out his arm but got a surprise. It hurt to move.

Plastic Frog didn't say anything. He sipped on his tropical juice drink, wearing his big hat and sunglasses. He was enjoying his time away from fighting crime.

Plastic Man tried stretching his foot into a big umbrella to shield himself from the hot sunshine. **"Ouch, ouch, ouch!"** he cried.

"Let me help," said Plastic Frog. He stretched an arm far over the beach.

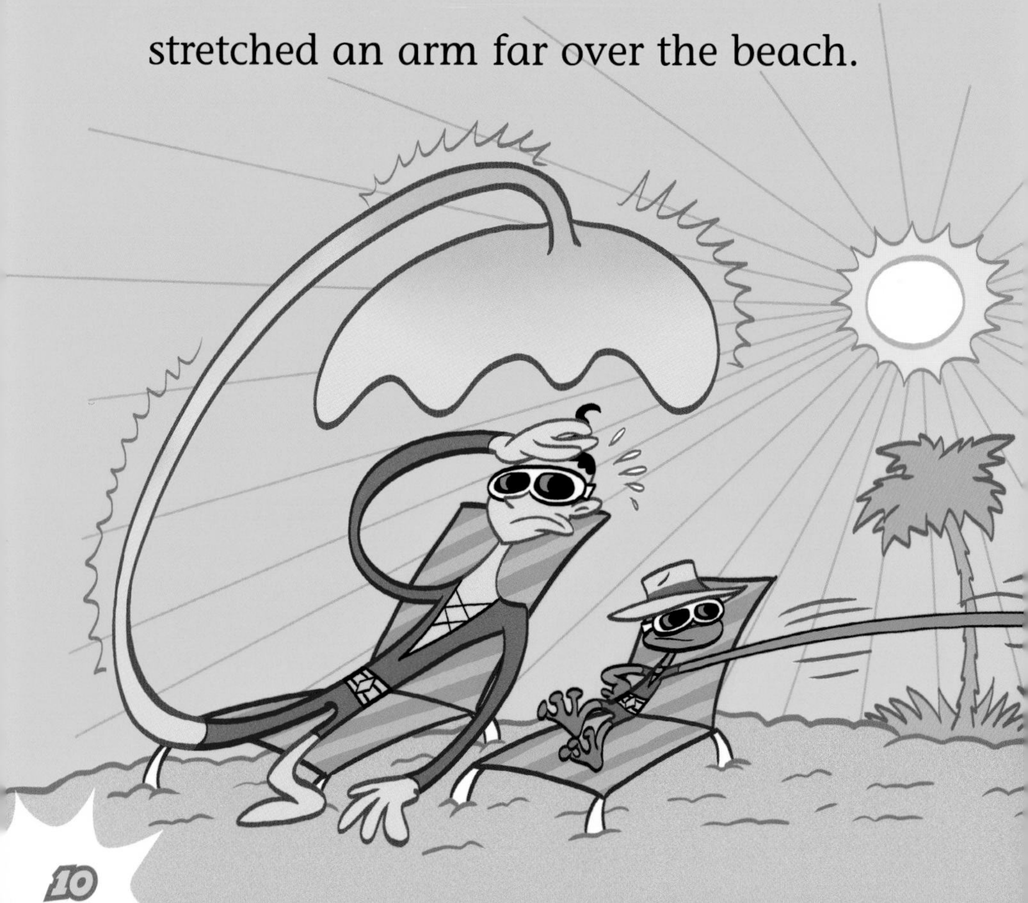

It stretched past sunbathers and rows of beach umbrellas. It stretched toward their hotel and reached into their room on the third floor. Then it grabbed a bottle of sunscreen.

ZING! His hand quickly zipped back.

Plastic Frog held out the lotion to Plastic Man.

"Ouch!" It hurt Plastic Man to even touch the bottle. "Maybe I'd better go inside," he said. "But just for a while."

He stood up from his lounge chair. "See you poolside, Plazzy," he said. "Ouch, ouch, ouch!" He walked painfully toward the hotel.

"Ah, what a perfect day," said Plastic Frog.

 A fly hummed overhead.

Plastic Frog's tongue stretched out and nabbed the insect.

The super frog smiled. "I know I should wait half an hour after eating," he told himself. "But I think it's time for another dip." Besides stretching and flexing, the little amphibian was an expert at swimming, too.

Plastic Frog removed his sombrero and sunglasses. He took one last sip of his juice drink. Then he rubbed his hands together, bent his knees, and jumped toward the water.

Plastic Frog hit a pile of wet sand.

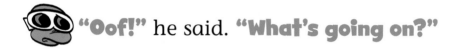 **"Oof!"** he said. **"What's going on?"**

He looked around and saw other swimmers wondering the same thing. The water was gone! They were all standing in a big, empty, muddy hole.

What had happened to Costa Tico's famous lagoon? Plastic Frog wondered.

He was wiping mud from his head when he saw footprints in the sand. And tail prints.

He zoomed his eyeballs in for a closer look. "Those prints belong to that creepy crook — **Kroc!**" said Plastic Frog. "That rotten reptile must have something to do with the missing water!"

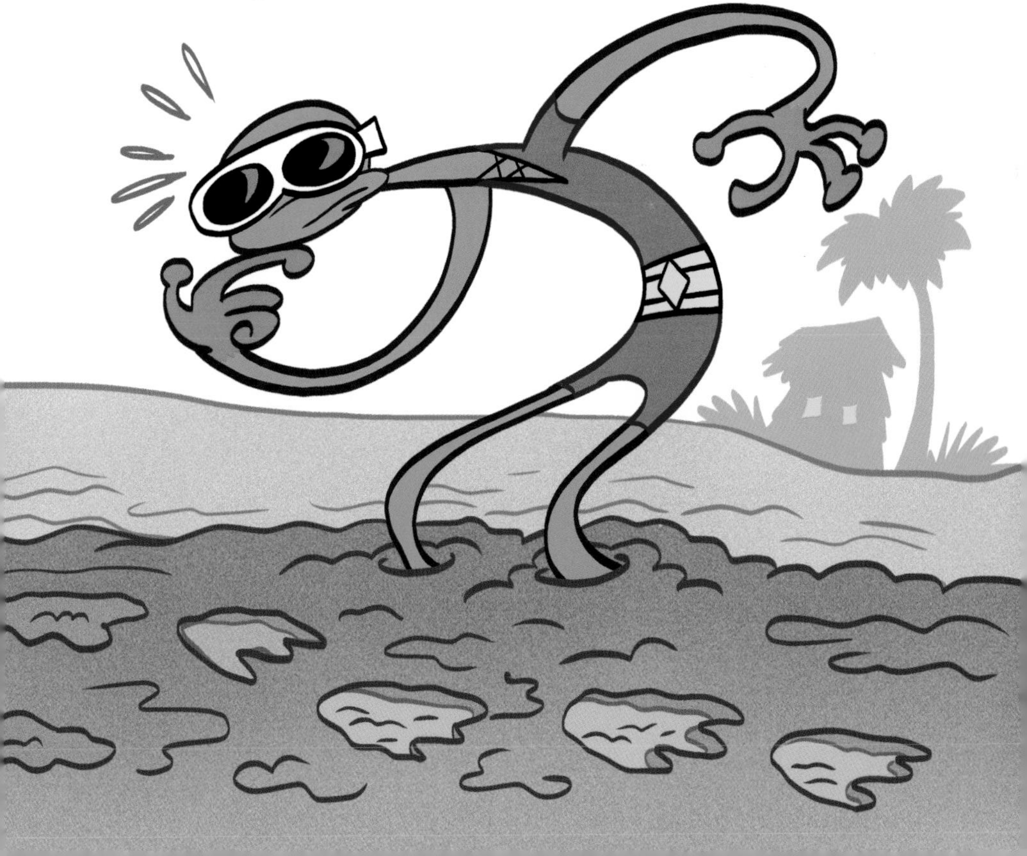

Plastic Frog looked back at his hotel. Plastic Man was not in top crime-fighting condition right now. He couldn't use his stretchy powers because of his painful sunburn.

The stretchy frog flexed his legs and arms. **He would have to take care of the crooked crocodile criminal all by himself.**

Z-BBBBBING!

Plastic Frog disappeared into the nearby forest with a powerful jump.

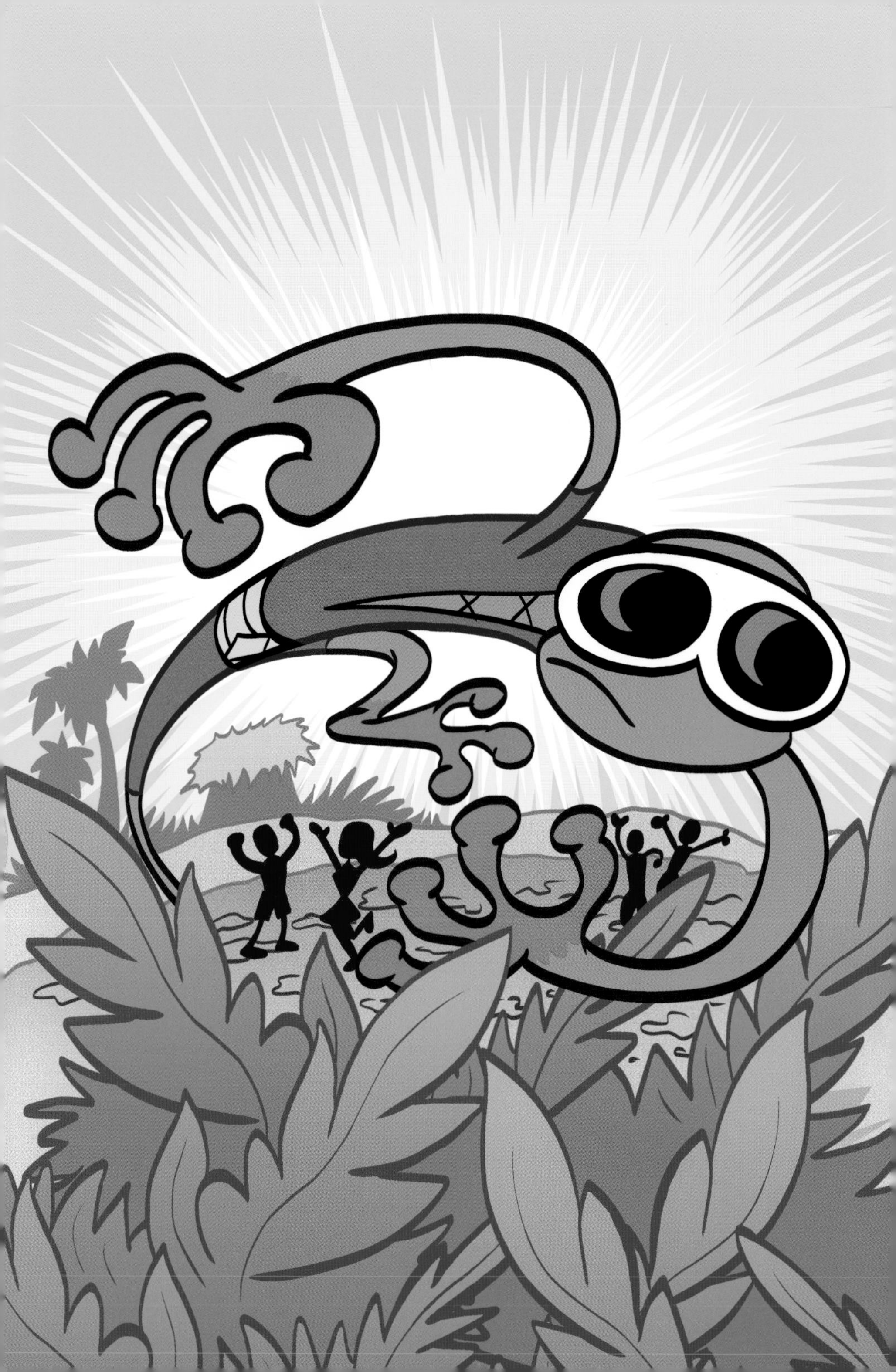

Chapter 2

TRICKS AND TRAPS

Plastic Frog bounced through the thick trees. He stretched out his long, long legs and pushed high into the air with each jump.

BOING! As he followed Kroc's trail, Plastic Frog kept his eyes open.

He knew that the rainforest could be a dangerous place. He had grown up in a forest just like this one many years ago.

When he was still a young frog, he liked to climb. One day, during a tropical storm, Plastic Frog had climbed up a very tall tree. A rubber tree. The rain had poured down. The thunder had boomed.

Suddenly, a bolt of lighting sizzled through the air.

The bolt struck the rubber tree. Somehow, the lightning, the rubber, and the little frog's slimy skin all got mixed up together. Ever since that day, Plastic Frog was able to stretch his body to amazing lengths.

As soon as he met Plastic Man, the two of them started fighting crime together. Just like today.

As he bounced along, Plastic Frog asked himself, **"Why would Kroc steal the lagoon water?"** 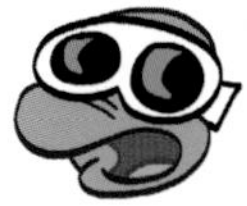

The crocodile's trail vanished into a wide, muddy river. Plastic Frog hopped over and stretched his neck above the water for a closer look.

"Hmmm, why didn't he steal this water, too?" Plastic Frog wondered.

A fish jumped up at Plastic Frog, its mouth wide open. Then more and more fish jumped out of the water straight at the stretchy frog.

All the fishes' mouths were full of deadly teeth.

Piranhas! thought Plastic Frog.

The Super-Pet was startled. He began to lose his balance. Quickly, the flexy frog stretched his body into a wide sail.

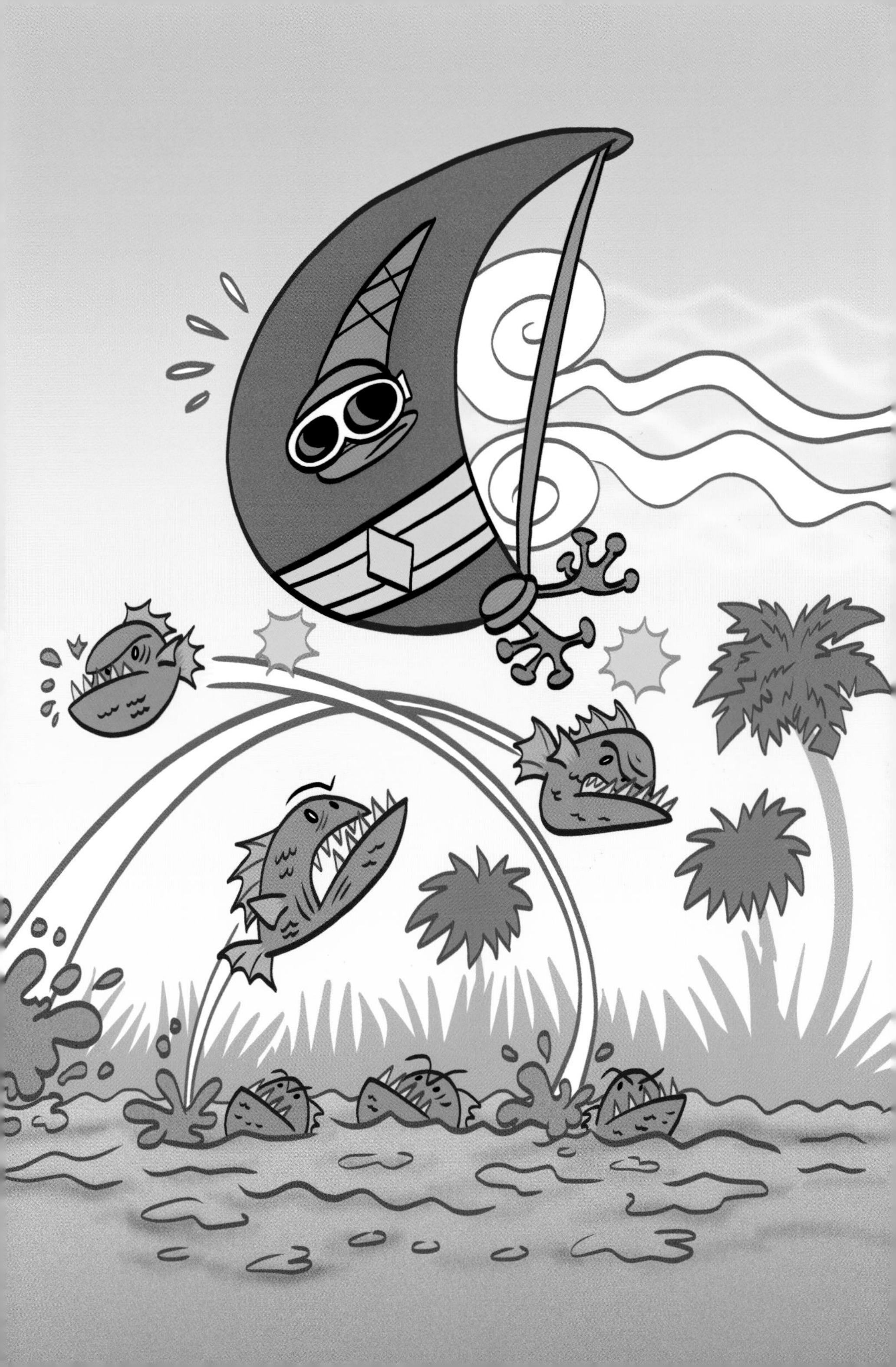

The wind puffed against his body and lifted him high above the fearsome fish. Then the breeze blew him to the other side of the river.

"Kroc only pretended to go in the water," said Plastic Frog. **"I have to be more careful about his tricks."** 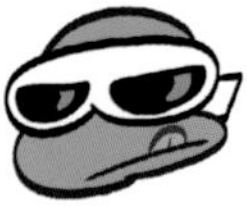

Plastic Frog continued through the forest. He found Kroc's trail again. This time it led through a thick grove of trees. Yellow blossoms and bright berries hung from the branches. Plastic Frog was getting hungry.

I should have finished my juice drink, he thought.

Then Plastic Frog heard a funny sound. ZZZZZ! A dart zoomed past his ear.

"Dart-berry trees! " he said. "I heard about these when I was a tadpole."

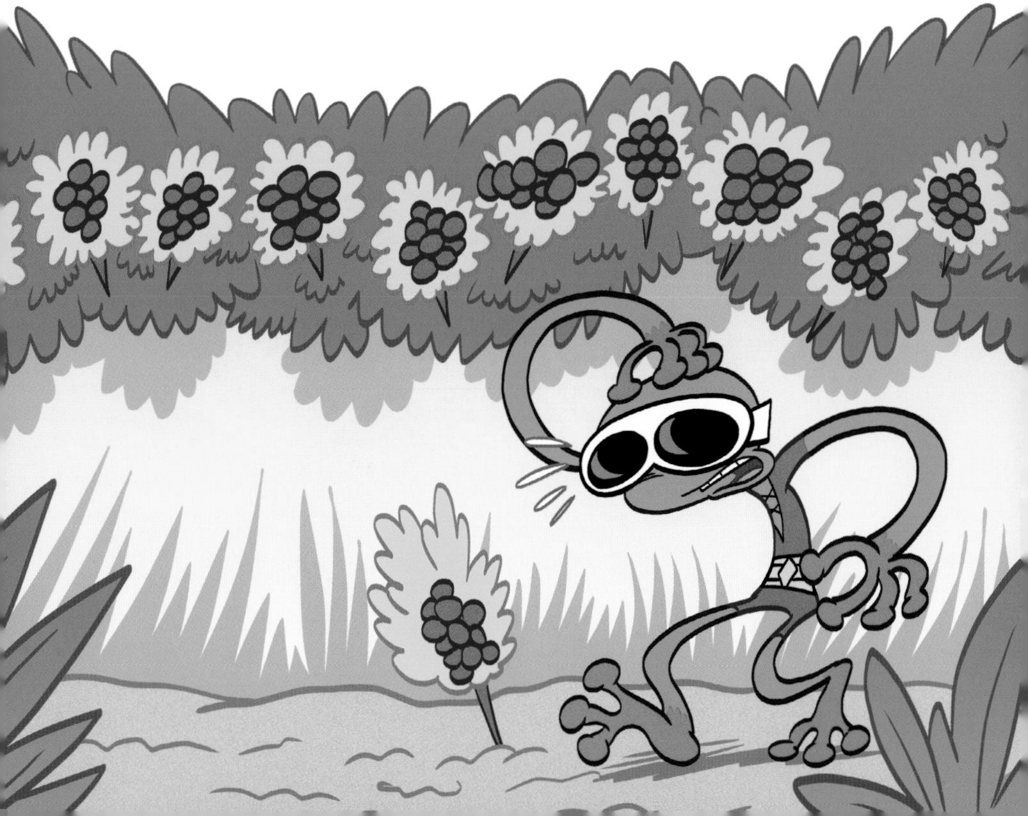

ZIP! ZAP! ZOOP!

More and more darts shot from the bright berries. Plastic Frog was surrounded. One poke from a single tip and Plastic Frog knew he would fall asleep — for days!

The stretchy frog used his bendy body to dodge the deadly darts. Up and down he stretched. He dipped and dived and twisted and turned.

"I haven't played with darts for a long time," he said. 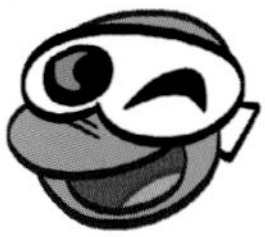

When all the berries were empty of darts, Plastic Frog collapsed to the ground.

Oof! I'll bet Kroc crawled through here on purpose, he thought, trying to catch his breath.

Plastic Frog spotted more footprints on the ground. They led toward a dark cave. The amphibian figured it must be the crook's hideout.

ZNNNAP!

His legs and arms snapped back into shape. **"Now I'm ready for that agua snatcher!"** he said. 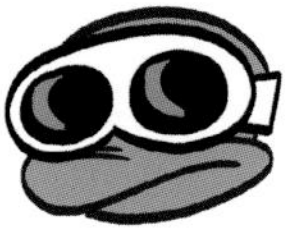

Carefully, Plastic Frog crept into the cave. It was quiet and cool inside. He could see a light at the far end of the tunnel.

A familiar voice echoed through the cave. Plastic Frog knew right away it belonged to greedy Kroc. "We'll be millionaires! We'll be billionaires!" Then a slithery voice replied, "No, we'll all be baz-z-z-z-z-z-zillionaires!"

Plastic Frog stretched forward on his silent rubbery feet. It took him only one step to reach the end. Then he stretched his head around the opening.

There was Kroc! And next to him was the **longest, biggest snake Plastic Frog had ever seen.**

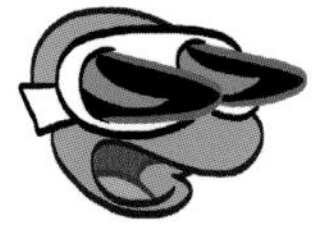

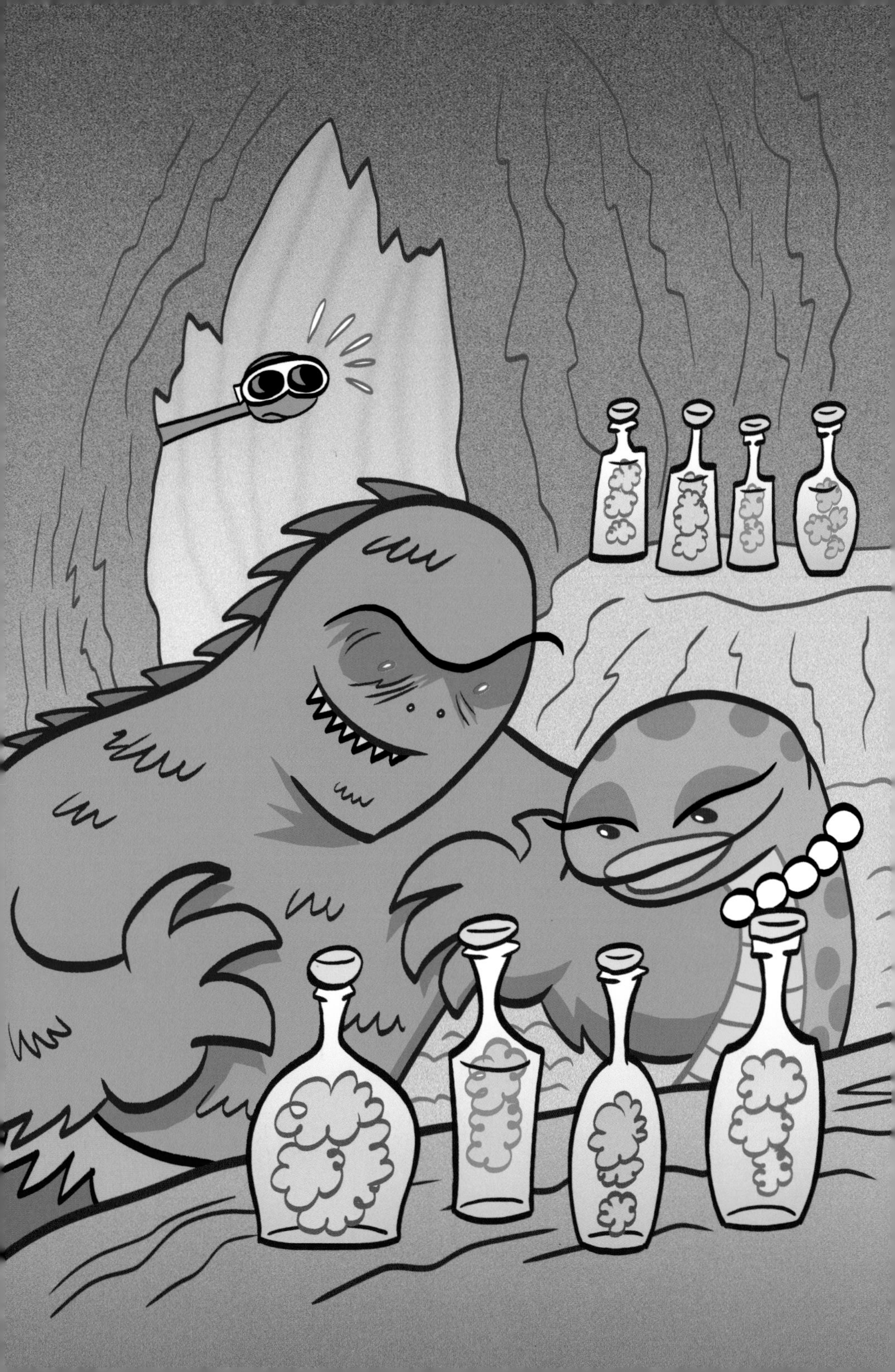

Growing up in the rainforest, Plastic Frog knew that snakes and frogs were enemies. The giant serpent and Kroc were looking at a row of glass bottles in all different shapes and sizes.

"People will pay us plenty for these," said Kroc, chuckling.

Crazy, thought Plastic Frog. *He's crazy. Those bottles are empty.*

Kroc and the snake had their backs to Plastic Frog. The super hero knew this was his chance.

ZOING! He bounced toward the two crooks. He stretched out his arms to grab them. BWOI-OI-OING!

Plastic Frog froze in midair. He couldn't move. Kroc turned to look at him. The crook laughed an evil laugh.

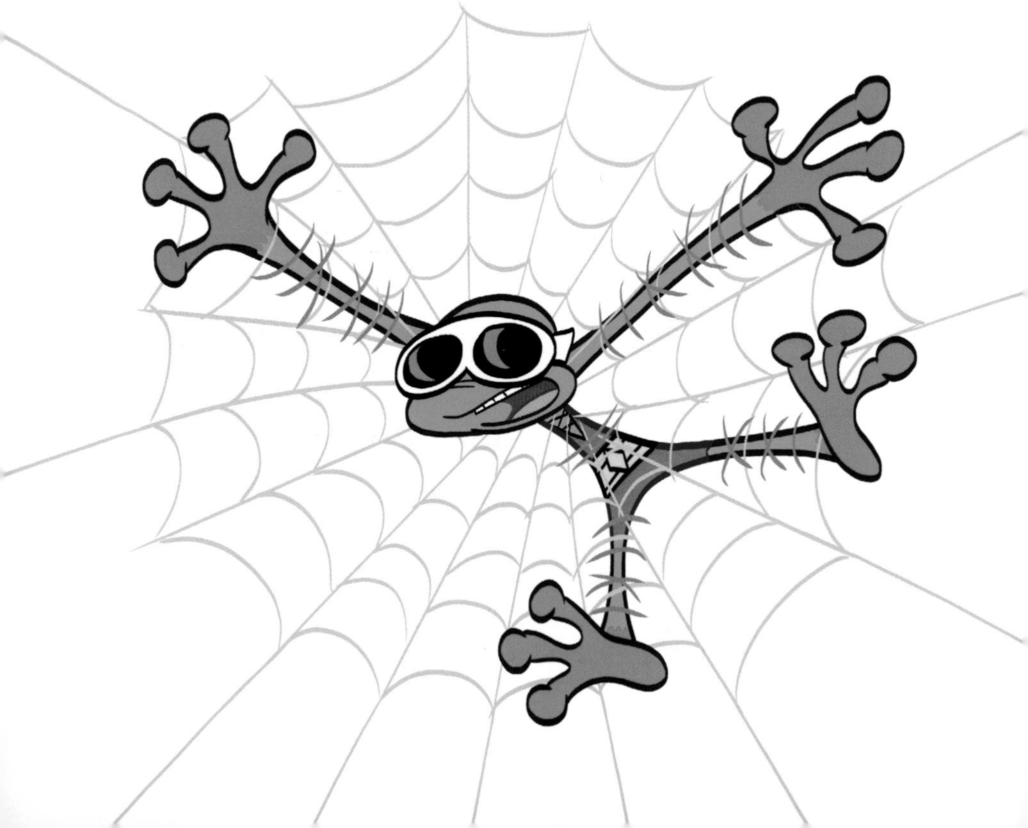

Chapter 3

WEB OF EVIL

Plastic Frog was trapped in a huge spider web. The strings of the web were as thin as wire. They were almost invisible. A giant spider floated down from the ceiling of the room. He was wearing a lab coat and thick glasses.

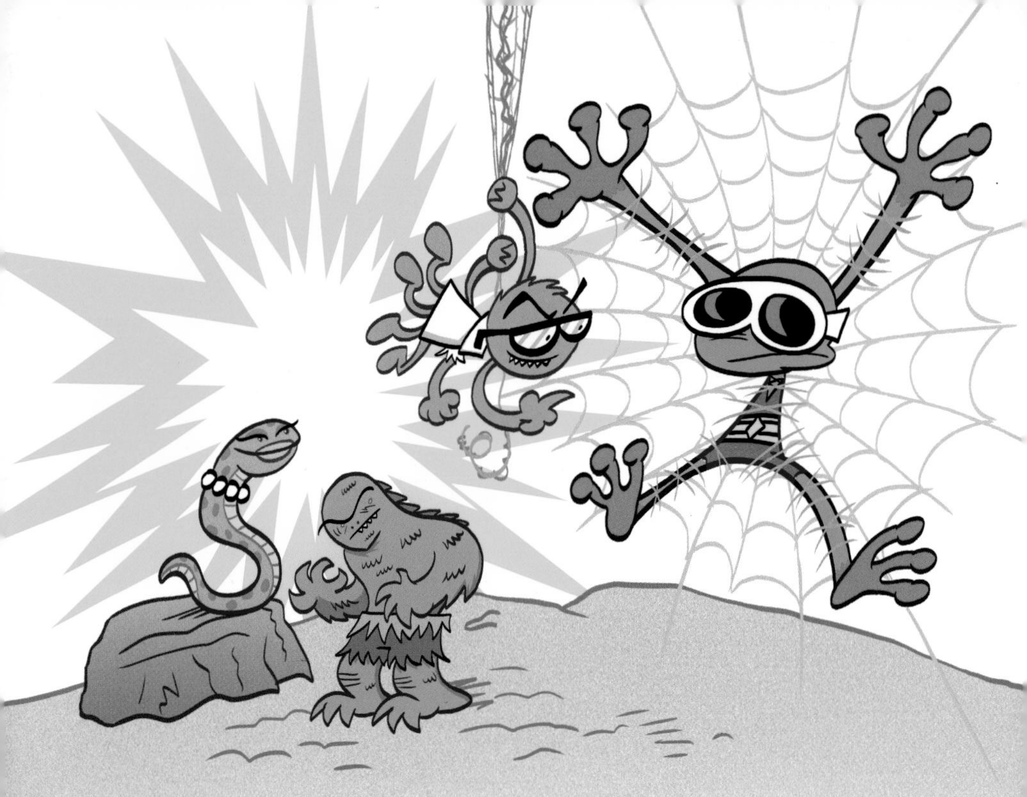

"I told you my trap would work," the spider said to Kroc. "Just in case anyone followed you from the lagoon."

Kroc smiled. "You certainly did, **Dr. Spider.** And now no matter how Plastic Frog stretches, he can't escape."

It was true. When Plastic Frog tried to stretch his arms and legs, the spider web stretched with him. And the web was so gooey, he could only stretch a little. Then he would snap back to his normal size. He was stuck good!

"Why did you steal the water from the lagoon?" Plastic Frog demanded.

"That's not all I stole," said the evil reptile. "Do you see these bottles? This one's the Gulf of Mexico. Here's the Panama Canal. These two over here hold the Amazon River."

"You're crazy," said Plastic Frog. "Those bottles are empty."

The huge snake hissed. "They only s-s-seem empty," she said. "The water has been turned into s-s-steam."

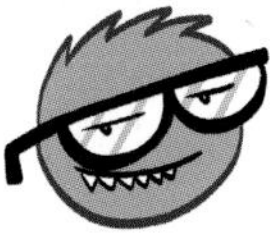

"I call it Spider Vapor," said Dr. Spider. He wriggled over to a machine in the middle of the room. "It's my own invention," he said. "This vaporizer lets me turn any body of water into a little cloud. Then Kroc and **Anna Conda** here can capture the cloud in one of my special bottles."

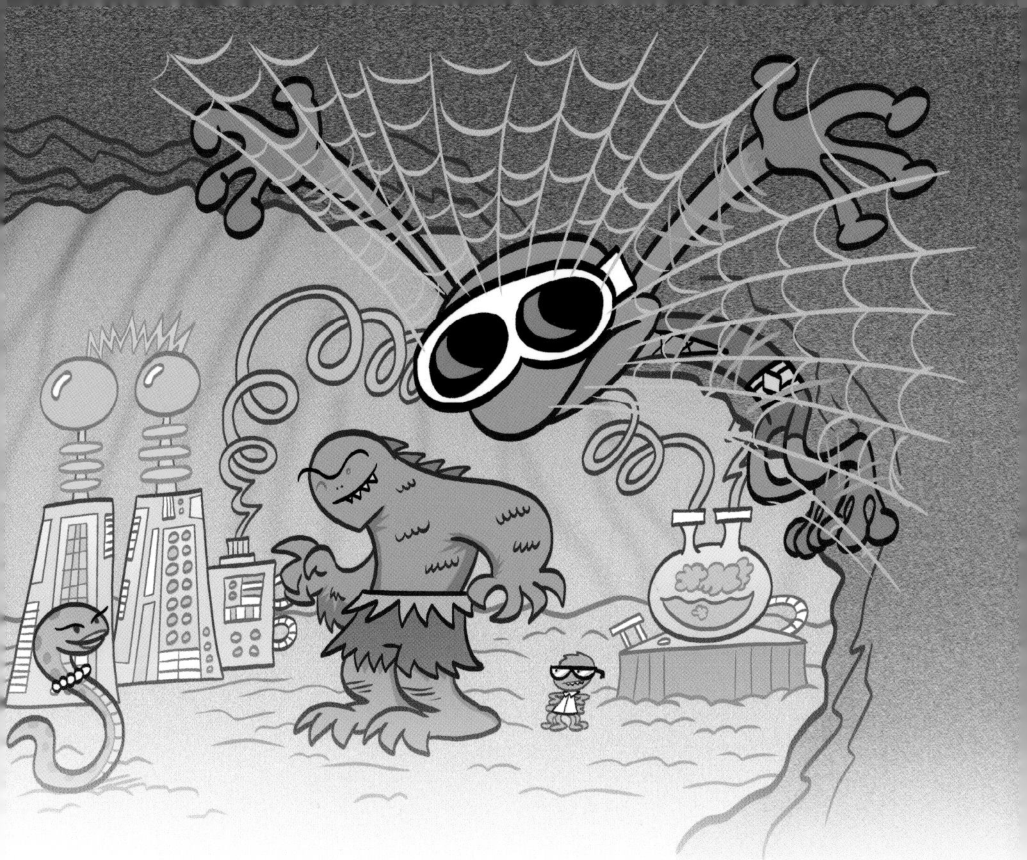

"Soon," said Kroc, "I will own the oceans and rivers of the world. And the humans will pay me anything I want to get them back. HAHAHA!"

"You mean, *we* will own them," said the spider. 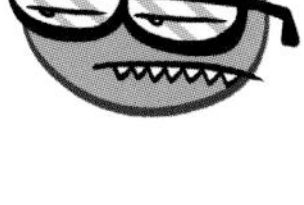

Anna Conda looked at Plastic Frog. Her tongue flickered in and out of her wide mouth. "I'm going to need a little snack," she said.

"Not so fast," said Dr. Spider. "I need you to handle one more bottle for me. The biggest one, yet. It's for the Pacific Ocean. After that, we'll be finished."

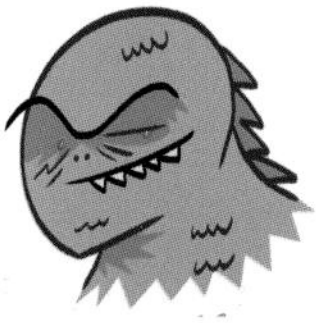

"Then we can start cashing in on my plan," said Kroc.

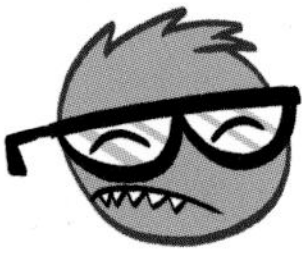

"You mean, *my* plan," said Dr. Spider coldly.

 **"It was my s-s-suggestion,"** hissed Anna Conda.

Those greedy goons! thought Plastic Frog. ***While they're arguing, I need to get free. But how?*** The web was too sticky. His arms and legs were stuck tight.

Plastic Frog did not want to end up as a snake snack. His stomach growled. The thought of food made him hungry. "I knew I should have finished that juice box," he told himself. "That furry fly was not enough."

Fly? Of course, that's how he could escape. The one part of his body that was not trapped by the web was his powerful tongue!

ZING! The frog's rubbery tongue zoomed out. It sailed over the heads of the arguing crooks. It grabbed onto the far end of the room.

Then Plastic Frog used the tongue to pull his whole body toward the wall. Inch by inch, Plastic Frog pulled himself forward. The web sticking to him was pulled too.

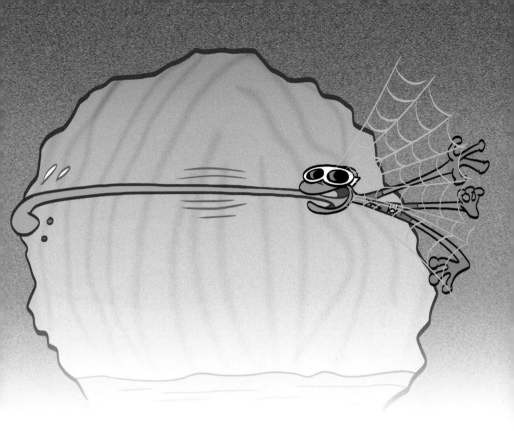

The web stretched tighter and

tighter. Then . . . Plastic Frog let go.

The web flipped loose. Plastic

Frog was launched like a stone in a

slingshot.

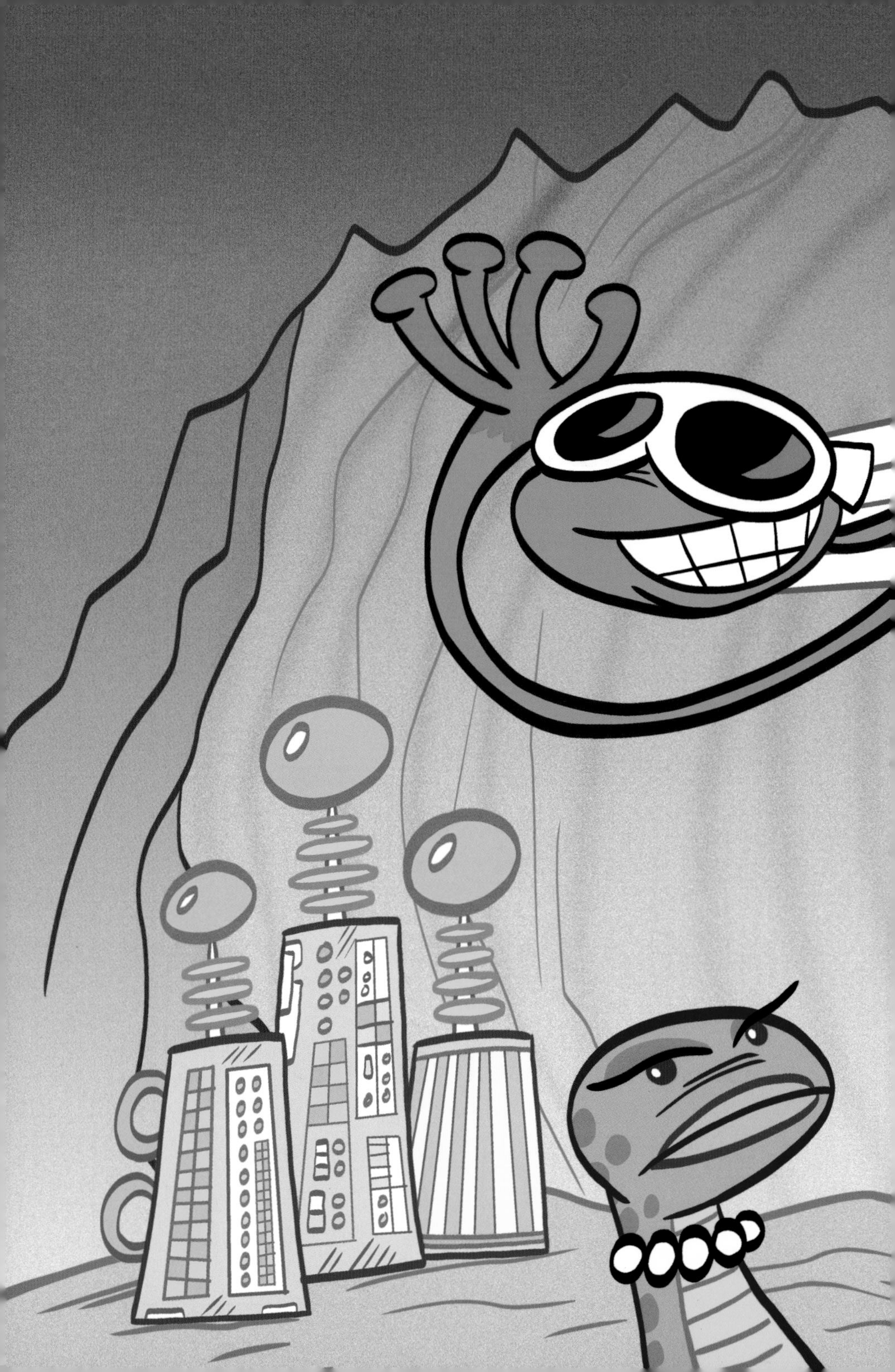

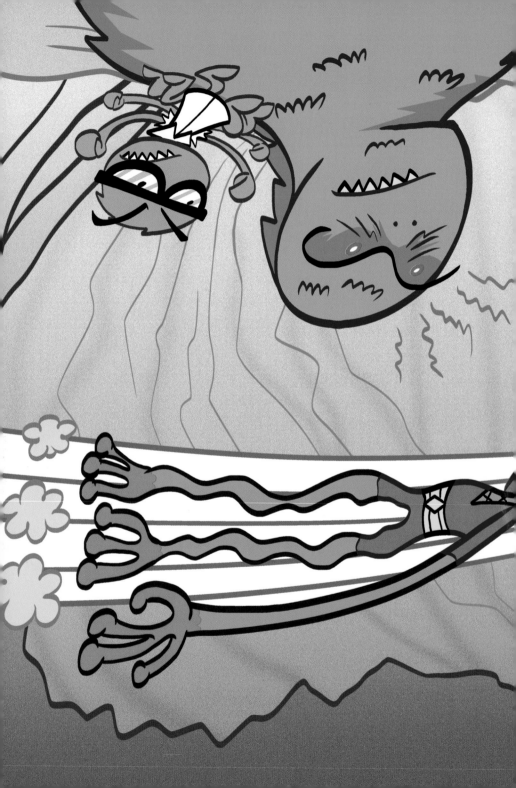

Plastic Frog sailed free of the sticky web. Then he stretched out his arms and grabbed onto the machine.

"Stop that do-gooder!" croaked Kroc.

All three crooks jumped at the frog. His bendy body slipped free. Anna Conda reached toward him. Plastic Frog kept twisting round and round the machine. The snake followed him. Round and round, faster and faster.

ZWINGGG! The dizzy snake couldn't catch the rubbery frog.

When the Super-Pet stopped twisting, the snake was tied in dozens of knots around the machine.

"Don't move!" Kroc shouted at Anna Conda. "You'll destroy my machine!"

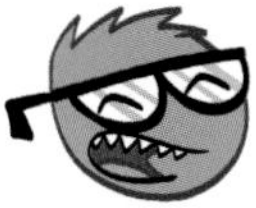

"My machine!" said Dr. Spider.

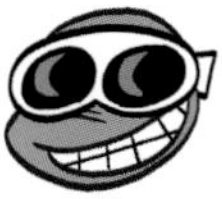

"Don't worry," said Plastic Frog. "I'll be the one to destroy your machine. But before I do, it has one last job."

Plastic Frog latched onto the vaporizer's controls. He flipped a switch, and the terrible trio all shouted.

Plastic Frog grabbed the empty bottle that was supposed to hold the Pacific Ocean. He opened the lid. Three clouds of steam were sucked inside. The villains were trapped, turned into vapor by their own evil machine.

Plastic Frog flexed his arms. He

stared at the clouds inside the bottle.

 **"You guys need to cool off,"**

he said. **"You look a little steamed!"**

*　　*　　*

Plastic Frog returned to his hotel.

Hours later, he and Plastic Man, who

had recovered from his sunburn,

returned the bodies of water to their

rightful places. They stretched across

deserts and mountains and cities to

restore the stolen liquid.

But Plastic Frog kept the bottle that held Kroc and his companions.

Soon, Plastic Frog and Plastic Man were stretched out on chairs by the lagoon again. This time, Plastic Man was wearing extra sunscreen.

"Ah, this is the perfect vacation spot," sighed Plastic Man.

"Yeah," agreed Plastic Frog. He sipped on a juice box and looked at the bottle next to him. **"It's a real gas!"**

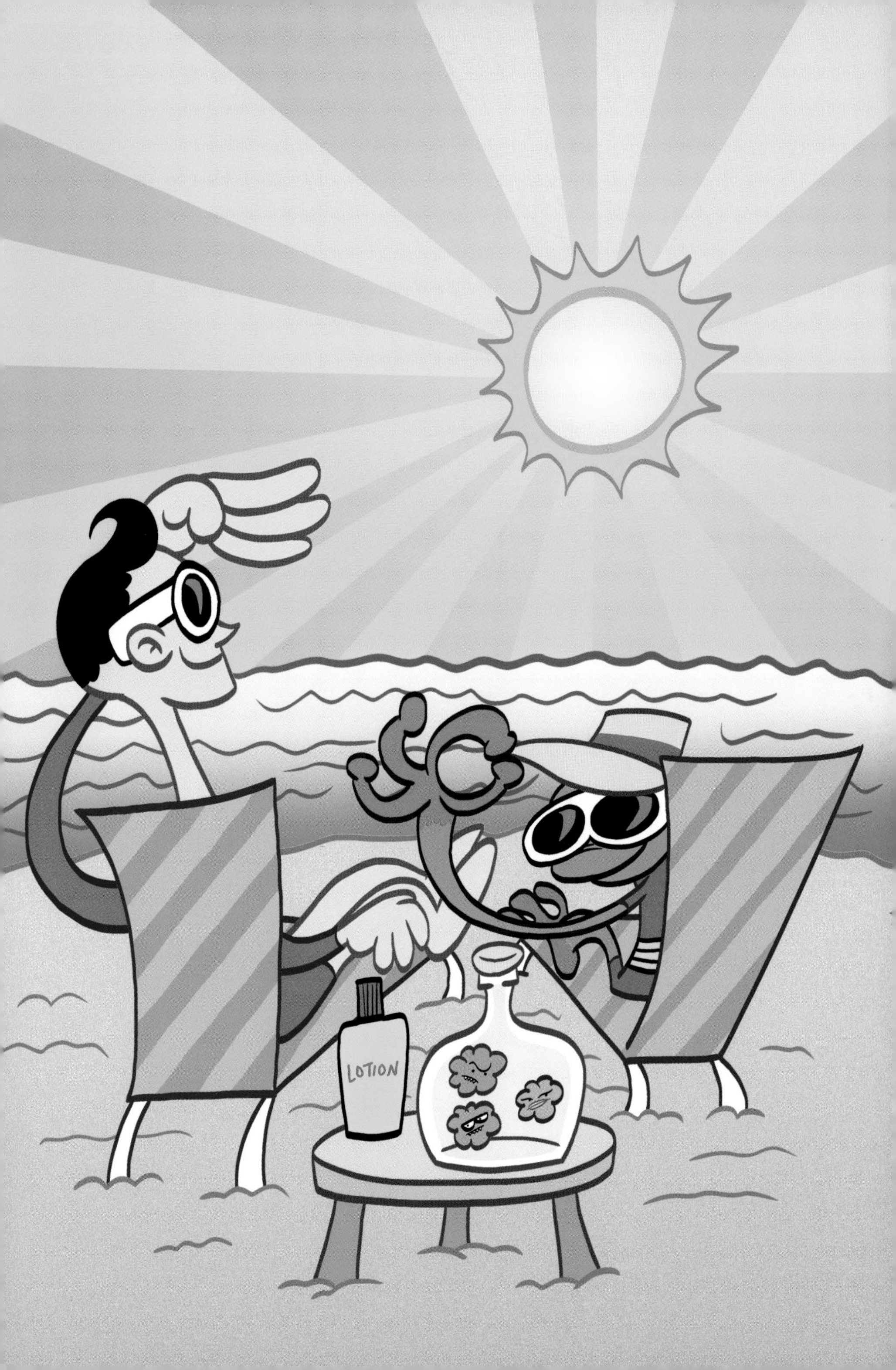
LOTION

KNOW YOUR HERO PETS!

1. Krypto
2. Streaky
3. Whizzy
4. Comet
5. Beppo
6. Super-Turtle
7. Fuzzy
8. Ace
9. Robin Robin
10. Batcow
11. Jumpa
12. Whatzit
13. Hoppy
14. Tawky Tawny
15. Spot
16. Plastic Frog
17. Gleek
18. Big Ted
19. Dawg
20. Space Dolphins
21. Proty
22. Chameleon Collie
23. Bull Dog
24. Paw Pooch
25. Tusky Husky
26. Hot Dog
27. Tail Terrier
28. Mammoth Mutt
29. Prophetic Pup
30. Rex the Wonder Dog
31. Detective Chimp
32. Starlene
33. Mossy
34. Merle
35. Loafers
36. Storm
37. Topo
38. Ark
39. Fluffy
40. Betty
41. Geoffrey
42. B'dg
43. Sen-Tag
44. Fendor
45. Stripezoid
46. Zallion
47. Ribitz
48. Bzzd
49. Gratch
50. Buzzoo
51. Fossfur
52. Zhoomp
53. Eeny

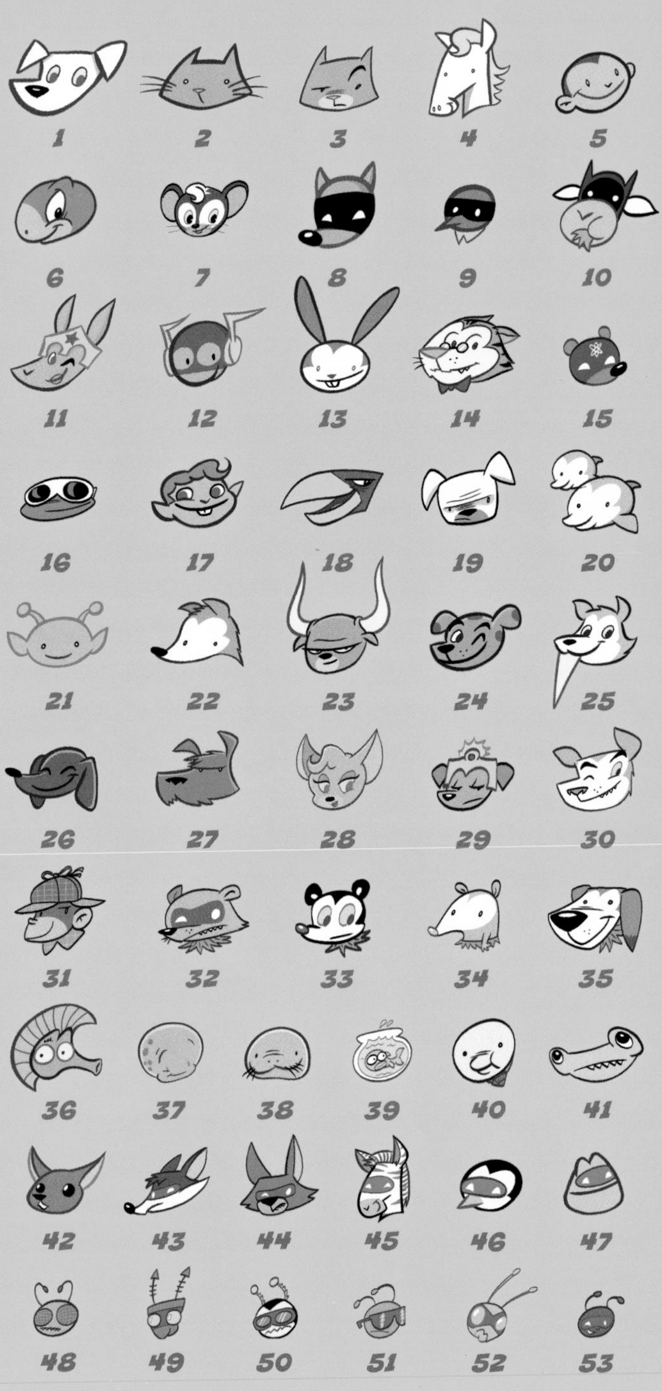

1
2
3
4
5
6
7
8
9
10
11
12
13
14
15
16
17
18
19
20
21
22
23
24
25
26
27
28
29
30
31
32
33
34
35
36
37
38
39
40
41
42
43
44
45
46
47
48
49
50
51
52
53

KNOW YOUR VILLAIN PETS!

1. Bizarro Krypto
2. Ignatius
3. Brainicat
4. Mechanikat
5. Dogwood
6. General Manx
7. Nizz
8. Fer-El
9. Crackers
10. Giggles
11. Artie Puffin
12. Griff
13. Waddles
14. Rozz
15. Mad Catter
16. Croward
17. Chauncey
18. Bit-Bit & X-43
19. Dr. Spider
20. Anna Conda
21. Mr. Mind
22. Sobek
23. Patches
24. Dex-Starr
25. Glomulus
26. Titano
27. Purring Pete
28. Kid Kitty
29. Scratchy Tom
30. Gat-Cat
31. Starro
32. Mama Ripples
33. Faye Precious
34. Limpy
35. Offie Lee
36. Misty
37. Sneezers
38. Johnny
39. Joey
40. Frankie
41. George
42. Whoosh
43. Pronto
44. Snorrt
45. Rolf
46. Squealer
47. Kajunn
48. Tootz
49. Eezix
50. Donald
51. Waxxee
52. Fimble
53. Webbik

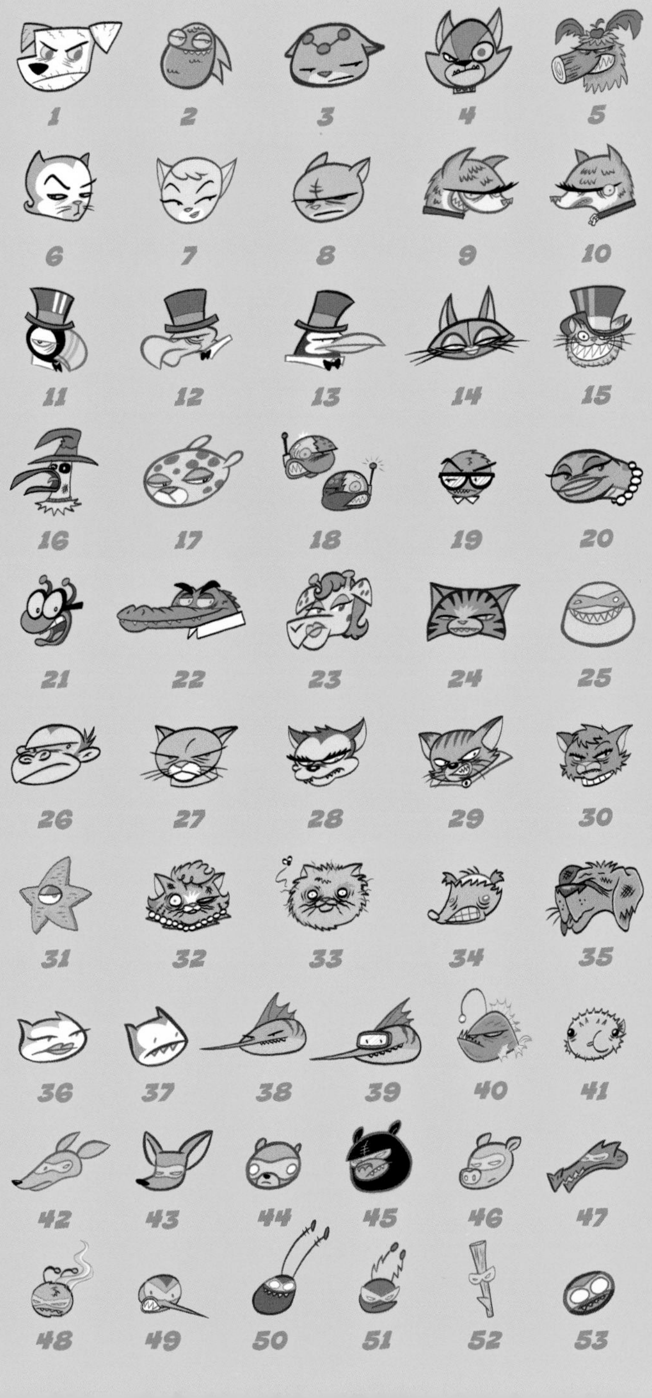
1 2 3 4 5
6 7 8 9 10
11 12 13 14 15
16 17 18 19 20
21 22 23 24 25
26 27 28 29 30
31 32 33 34 35
36 37 38 39 40 41
42 43 44 45 46 47
48 49 50 51 52 53

MEET THE AUTHOR!

Michael Dahl

When he's not writing, Michael cares for his pet, Tulsa, part Border Collie, part Catahoula Leopard Dog. She's so smart that she actually smiles for the camera! Michael is the author of the bestselling Library of Doom series, several DC Super Hero chapter books, and the Hocus Pocus Hotel mysteries.

MEET THE ILLUSTRATOR!

Eisner Award-winner Art Baltazar

Art Baltazar is a cartoonist machine from the heart of Chicago! He defines cartoons and comics not only as an art style, but as a way of life. Currently, Art is the creative force behind *The New York Times* best-selling, Eisner Award-winning, DC Comics series Tiny Titans, and the co-writer for *Billy Batson and the Magic of SHAZAM!* Art is living the dream! He draws comics and never has to leave the house. He lives with his lovely wife, Rose, big boy Sonny, little boy Gordon, and little girl Audrey. Right on!

WORD POWER!

amphibian (am-FIB-ee-uhn)—a cold-blooded animal with a backbone that is able to live both on land and in water, such as a frog, toad, or salamander

piranha (pi-RAH-nuh)—small flesh-eating South American freshwater fishes that have very sharp teeth

rainforest (RAYN-for-ist)—a dense, tropical forest where a lot of rain falls

reptile (REP-tile)—a cold-blooded, air-breathing animal with a backbone; reptiles usually lay eggs and have skin covered with scales or bony plates.

sombrero (som-BRER-oh)—a straw hat with a wide brim worn in Mexico and the southwestern United States

tropical (TROP-uh-kuhl)—having to do with the hot, rainy areas of the tropics

vaporizer (VAY-puh-rye-zuhr)—a device that turns water into gas

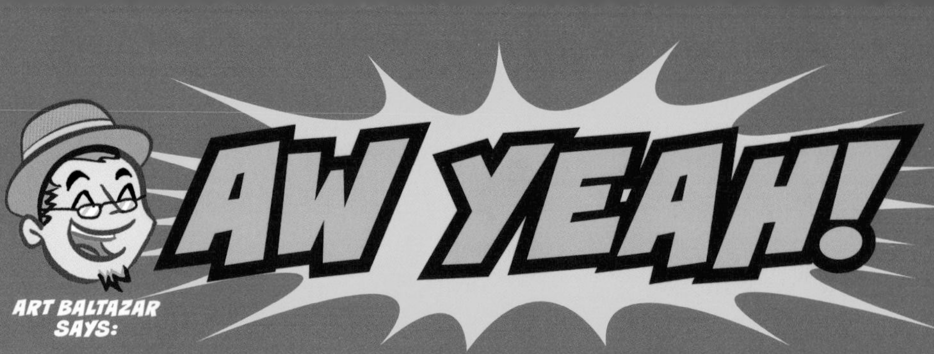
ART BALTAZAR
SAYS:
AW YEAH!

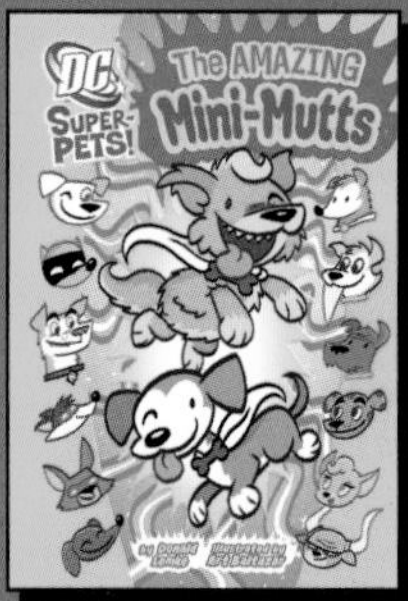
DC SUPER-PETS!
The AMAZING Mini-Mutts

HERO DOGS GALORE!

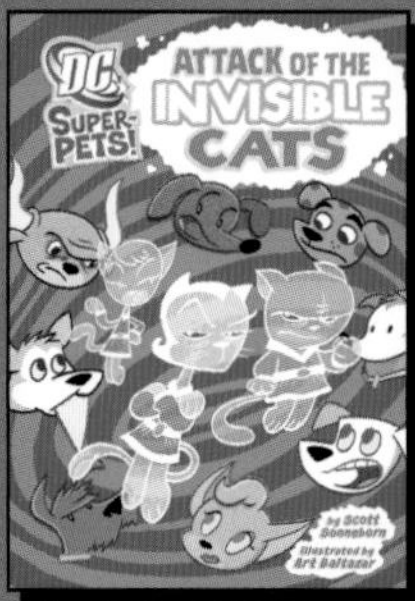
DC SUPER-PETS!
ATTACK OF THE INVISIBLE CATS
by Scott Sonneborn
illustrated by Art Baltazar

SPACE CANINE PATROL AGENCY!

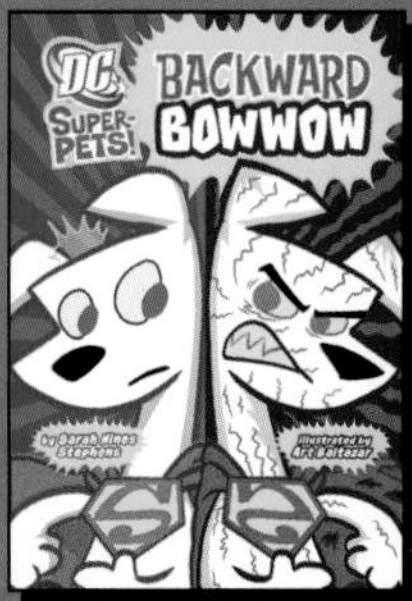
DC SUPER-PETS!
BACKWARD BOWWOW

KRYPTO THE SUPER-DOG!

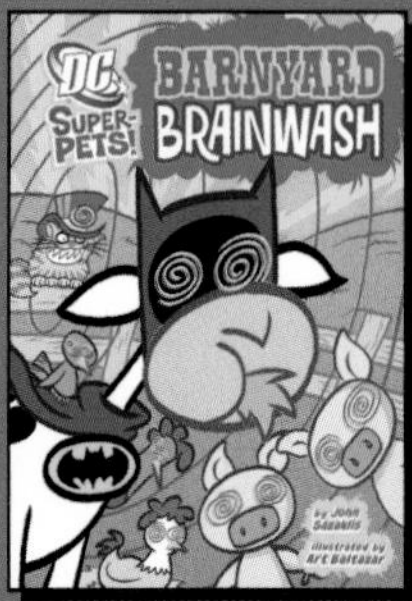
DC SUPER-PETS!
BARNYARD BRAINWASH

BATCOW!

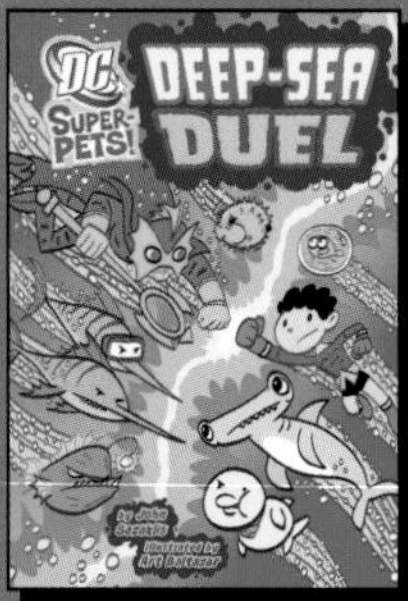
DC SUPER-PETS!
DEEP-SEA DUEL

FLUFFY AND THE AQUA-PETS!

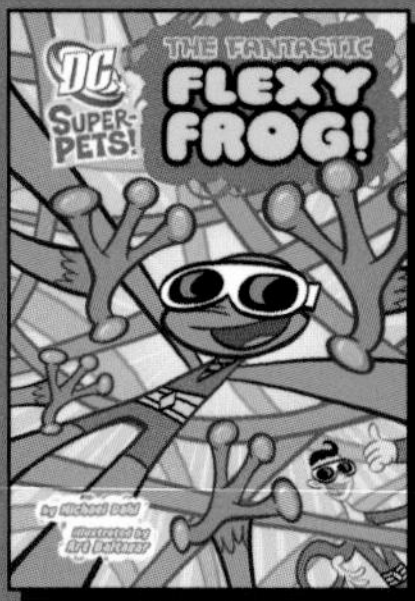
DC SUPER-PETS!
THE FANTASTIC FLEXY FROG!

PLASTIC FROG!

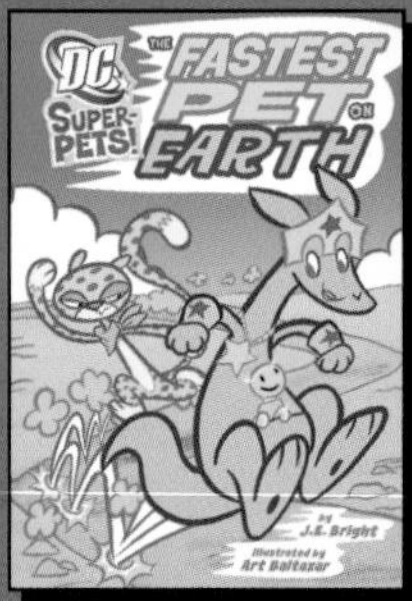
DC SUPER-PETS!
THE FASTEST PET ON EARTH
by J.E. Bright
illustrated by Art Baltazar

JUMPA THE KANGA!

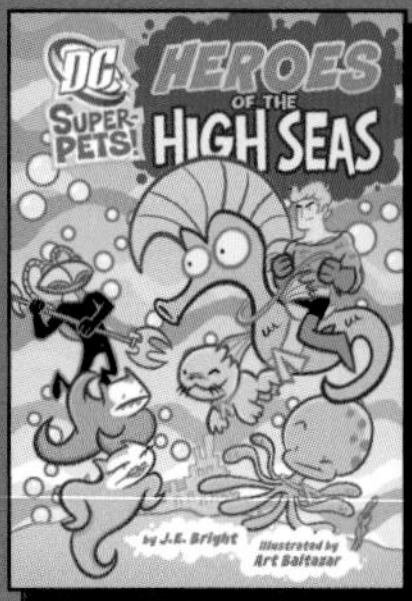
DC SUPER-PETS!
HEROES OF THE HIGH SEAS
by J.E. Bright
illustrated by Art Baltazar

STORM AND THE AQUA-PETS!

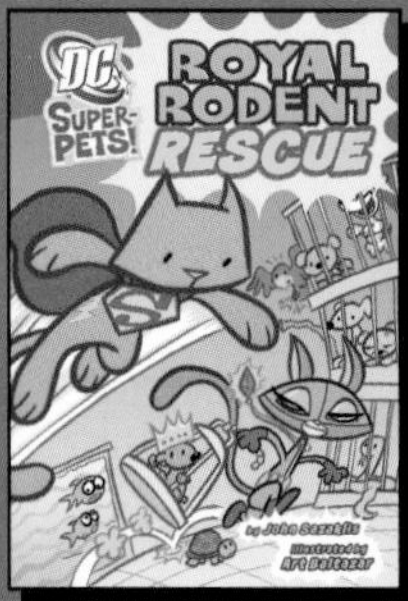
DC SUPER-PETS!
ROYAL RODENT RESCUE
by John Sazaklis
illustrated by Art Baltazar

STREAKY THE SUPER-CAT!

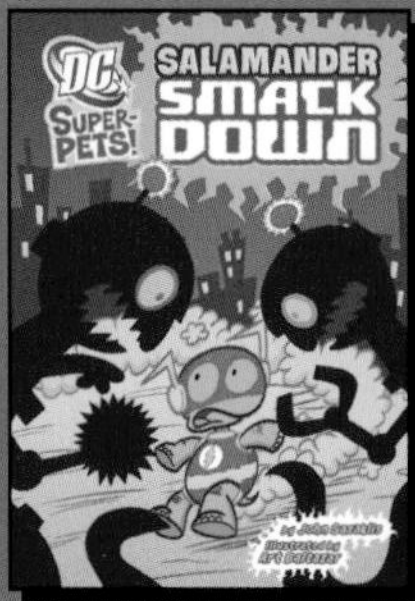
DC SUPER-PETS!
SALAMANDER SMACK DOWN

THE TERRIFIC WHATZIT!

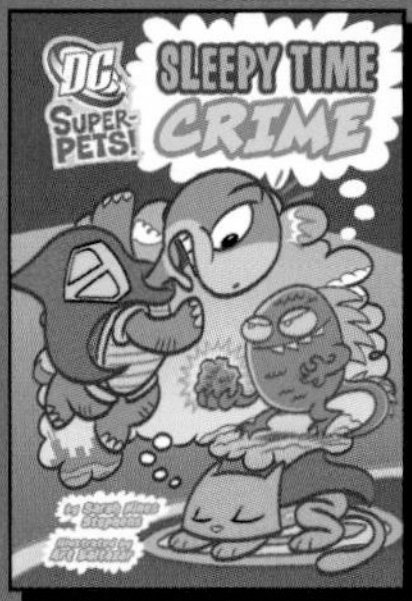
DC SUPER-PETS!
SLEEPY TIME CRIME

SUPER-TURTLE!

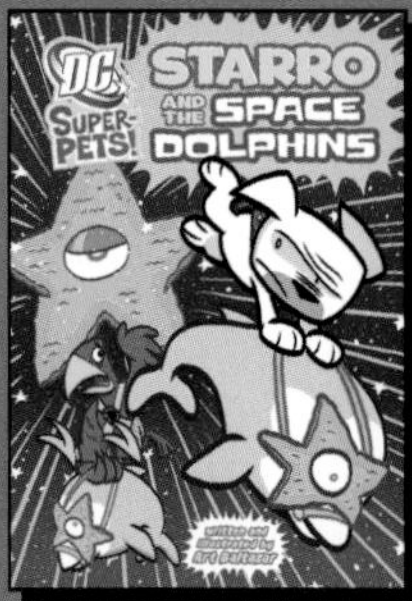
DC SUPER-PETS!
STARRO AND THE SPACE DOLPHINS

BIG TED AND DAWG!

Read all of these totally awesome stories today, starring all of your favorite DC SUPER-PETS!

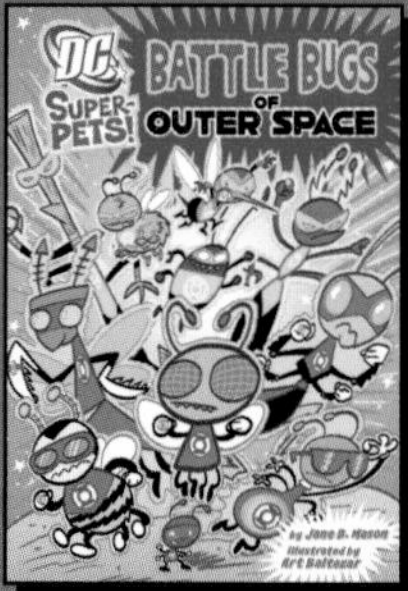
DC SUPER-PETS!
BATTLE BUGS OF OUTER SPACE
by Jane B. Mason
Illustrated by Art Baltazar

GREEN LANTERN BUG CORPS!

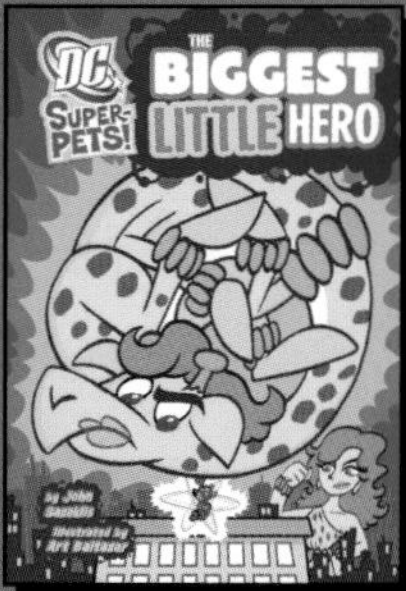
DC SUPER-PETS!
THE BIGGEST LITTLE HERO

SPOT!

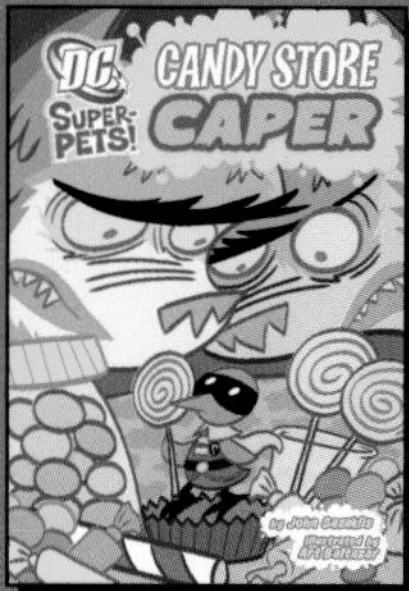
DC SUPER-PETS!
CANDY STORE CAPER
by John Sazaklis
Illustrated by Art Baltazar

ROBIN ROBIN AND ACE TEAM-UP!

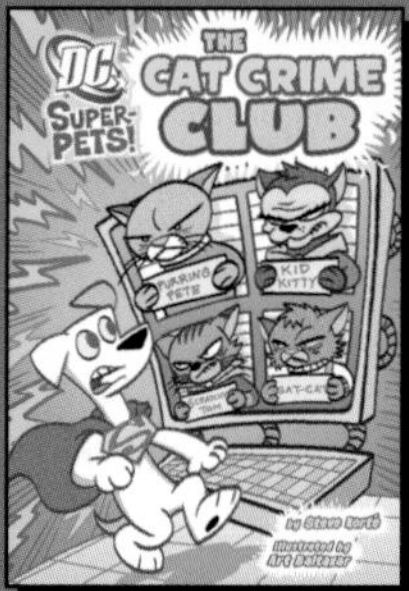
DC SUPER-PETS!
THE CAT CRIME CLUB
KID KITTY
by Steve Korté
Illustrated by Art Baltazar

SPACE CANINE PATROL AGENCY!

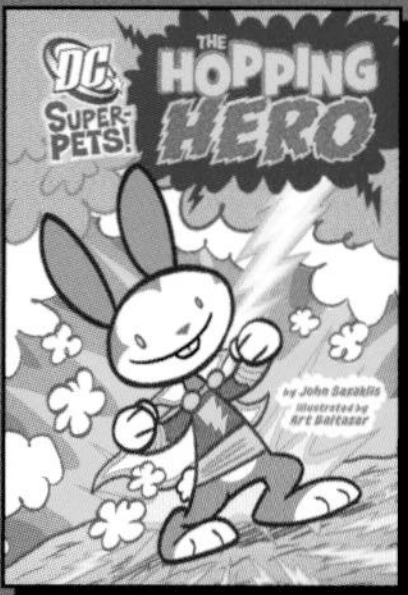
DC SUPER-PETS!
THE HOPPING HERO
by John Sazaklis
Illustrated by Art Baltazar

HOPPY!

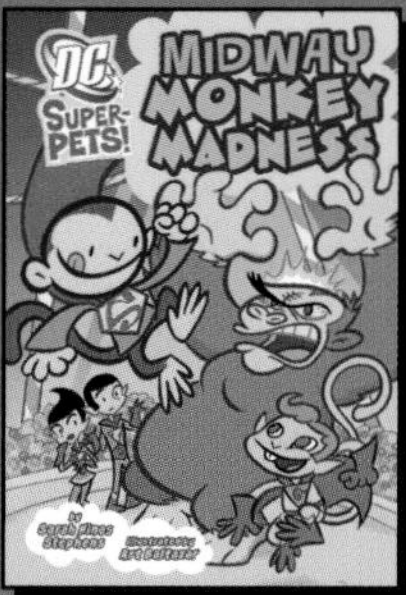
DC SUPER-PETS!
MIDWAY MONKEY MADNESS

BEPPO THE SUPER-MONKEY!

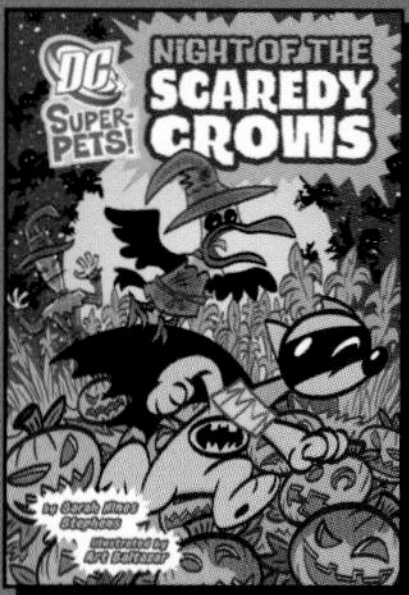
DC SUPER-PETS!
NIGHT OF THE SCAREDY CROWS

ACE THE BAT-HOUND!

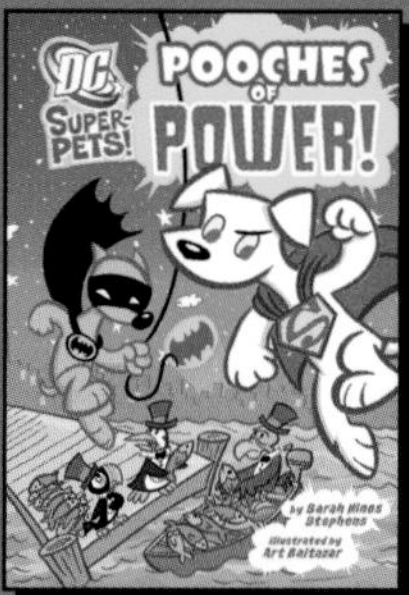
DC SUPER-PETS!
POOCHES OF POWER!
by Sarah Hines Stephens
Illustrated by Art Baltazar

KRYPTO AND ACE TEAM-UP!

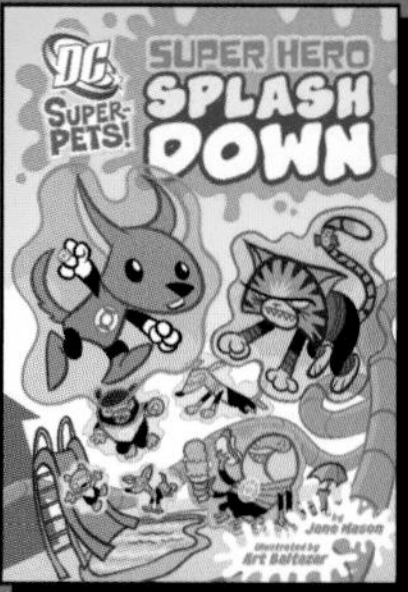
DC SUPER-PETS!
SUPER HERO SPLASH DOWN
by Jane Mason
Illustrated by Art Baltazar

B'DG, THE GREEN LANTERN!

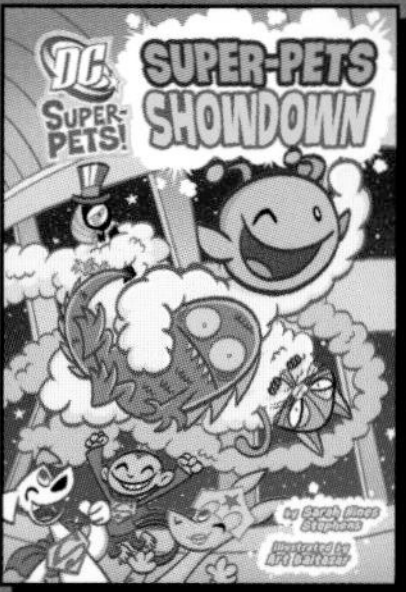
DC SUPER-PETS!
SUPER-PETS SHOWDOWN
by Sarah Hines Stephens
Illustrated by Art Baltazar

THE LEGION OF SUPER-PETS!

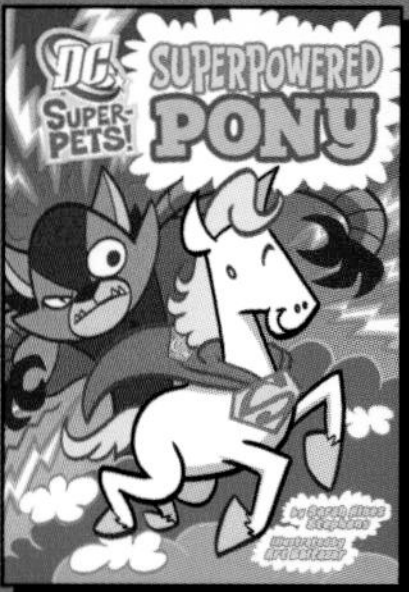
DC SUPER-PETS!
SUPERPOWERED PONY

COMET THE SUPER-HORSE!

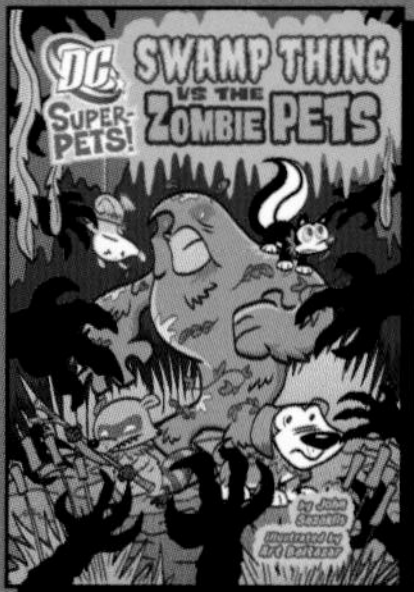
DC SUPER-PETS!
SWAMP THING VS THE ZOMBIE PETS
by John Sazaklis
Illustrated by Art Baltazar

DOWN HOME CRITTER GANG!

THE FUN DOESN'T STOP HERE!

Discover more:

- Videos & Contests!
- Games & Puzzles!
- Heroes & Villains!
- Authors & Illustrators!

@ www.capstonekids.com

Find cool websites and more books like this one at www.facthound.com Just type in Book I.D. 9781404864948 and you're ready to go!

Picture Window Books™

Published in 2012
A Capstone Imprint
1710 Roe Crest Drive
North Mankato, MN 56003
www.capstonepub.com

Cataloging-in-Publication Data is available
at the Library of Congress website.
ISBN: 978-1-4048-6494-8 (library binding)
ISBN: 978-1-4048-7666-8 (paperback)

Summary: On a tropical beach, Plastic Man
and his Super-Pet, Plastic Frog, stretch out
near a beautiful lagoon. But when the water
suddenly disappears, their dream vacation
becomes real nightmare! To save day, Plastic
Frog must flex his muscles and take down a
crafty croc and two wily water-snatchers.

Art Director & Designer: Bob Lentz
Editor: Donald Lemke
Creative Director: Heather Kindseth
Editorial Director: Michael Dahl

Printed in the United States of America
in Stevens Point, Wisconsin.
032012   006678WZF12

DC™

SUPER-PETS!

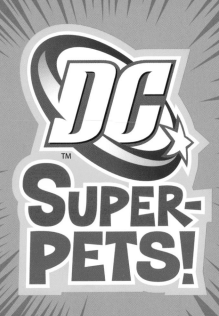

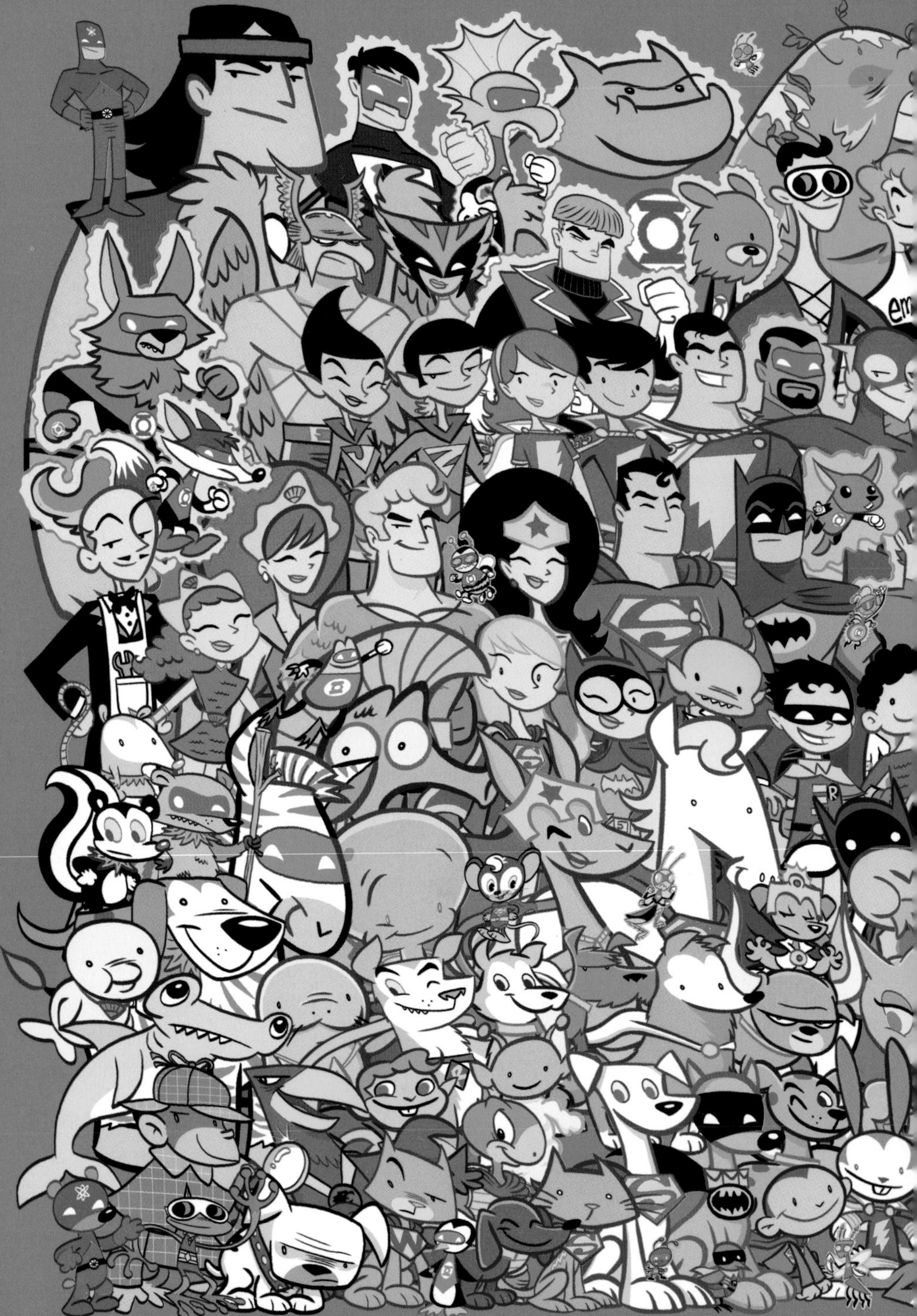